SOPHOMORE
FREAK

Book Two in the Reject High Series

Brian Thompson

ACKNOWLEDGEMENTS

To: My Lord and Savior Jesus Christ for the continual flow of ideas and the ability to do what I love.

To Heather, my wife, business partner, and sounding board. Thank you.

To my parents, Bradley and Barbara, for their continuing support and love.

To all those who contributed toward this work: my editing group and friends Jackie Rodriguez, Jeff Hipps, and Martha Brown of the East Metro Atlanta Christian Writers; my beta reading team Bethany Allmon, Laura Almond, Tamiko Bowman, Tiandria Cotton, Becca Cronk, Maureen Henn, Gina Johnston, Anna Oliver, Lisa Sinnock, Valerie Strawmier, Adrienne Thompson, DeAnna Troupe and Brittany Watkins – thank you for your input and feedback.

To my editor on this project, Mary Marvella; my friends and mentors Charles Clark, Tia McCollors, Tyora Moody, Kemya Scott and Cyrus Webb – thank you. Special thanks to Phyllis Conway, Matt Criswell, Debra Harley, Margaret Harley, the Lowe family, Christine Mayfield, Jeff and Diane Ransom, and Susan Scherffel for inspiring me.

To my pastor, Bishop Eddie L. Long for spiritual guidance and support.

Watch for *Forgotten,* the third book in the *Reject High* series, coming in summer, 2015.

CAST OF CHARACTERS
(in alphabetical order)

Joyce Anderson: Sasha's mother.

Sasha Anderson: Jason's girlfriend; can clone herself.

Debra Brown: Jason's legal guardian, Zachary's mother and Ray's ex-wife.

Ryan Cain: former student at Reject High; Jason broke his jaw.

Amauri Camuto: member of the Collective.

Jason Ray Champion, Sr.: Jason, Jr's and Zachary's father, goes by "Ray."

Jason Ray Champion, Jr.: former Reject High student. He is strong, invulnerable, and can jump immeasurable distances.

Vivienne Coker: head of Positive Growth troubled youth boot camp.

Esteban Hernandez: The youngest Hernandez triplet; Positive Growth camper.

Julio Hernandez: The oldest Hernandez triplet, works for David King.

Luis Hernandez: The middle Hernandez triplet, works for David King.

Solomon Hughes: member of the Collective.

Belinda King: school board chairman and David's sister.

David King: member of the Collective.

Deidra Lee: Jason's aunt; older sister of Anna.

Susan Lin: Jason's therapist.

George Lowe: Rhapsody's father, dying of bone cancer.

Rhapsody Lowe: Jason's best friend; can turn invisible and quantum tunnel or "ghost" her body through solid objects.

Ruby Martinez: Rhapsody's mother.

Julia Mosri-Champion: Ray's wife.

Jeff Peters: former Earth Science teacher at Reject High.

Michael Selby: Sasha's ex-boyfriend; can move at tremendous speeds.

Stuart Spivey: former Student Resource Officer at Reject High.

Eris Courtney Stafford: member of the Collective.

Ron Welker: ex-principal of Reject High; member of the Collective.

CHAPTER ONE

therapy gone wild

A warm, salty August breeze blew on my face. I blinked hard, my heart racing. On the floor to my left lay a huge chunk of splintered wood. Next to it were jagged metal hinge pieces alongside tiny glass fragments. I was near the ocean, somewhere on the west side of town in my therapist's office, or what was left of it.

I blacked out, a rage blackout – got angry and did a terrible amount of damage. Bile rose in my stomach. My throat was already dry, but suddenly it was tough to breathe. Susan, my psychologist for the past three years, was *gone*. I might have finally done it, lost control and killed someone I cared about.

Turning my hands over I examined them. I didn't see blood, but that didn't mean anything.

All the news stations would carry the story or would splash my shame for all to see. *Fifteen-year-old black teenager Jason Champion murdered psychologist Susan Lin.* The police would try to arrest me. I'd resist, and they would discover the secret I'd been keeping for the past three months.

Air drifted in from the beachfront window, drying the cold sweat on my back. I inhaled and held my breath to quell the nausea. Under normal circumstances, the wall-length glass didn't open. My gaze drifted over to what remained of it. In the distance a floating rectangle with a gold knob floated on the waves. I'd tossed a door a quarter of a mile away into the ocean. Was she out there with it?

"Susan?" I called out. I prayed she was alive. "You're okay, right? It's safe."

She didn't answer back.

I scrambled over to the windowpane, cupped my hands around my mouth, and shouted her name again. Was she drowning in the surf? Could she swim?

Susan wasn't in the storage closet, the mini-kitchen or dusty attic. Through the bathroom's window, I checked the parking lot. Her navy blue Shogun motorcycle was still there. Had she survived? Run out on foot? Called the cops?

I swallowed hard. I had to get out of here, but not before finding out the truth.

Little vivid details remained in my mind, like crumbs left over from something larger and more important. Susan had pushed me into talking about my dead mother and flipped my switch.

Then her slender white finger, the one with the tattooed ring on it, had pointed to the "danger room." (It's an enclosed area to protect her from those clients who go mental and need to let it out.) I'd raged in it before. Going inside would have worked two months ago, before I became invincible and ridiculously strong.

Maybe she was hiding. I hadn't checked her husband's office. It was locked, so I waited, listening for movement. Hearing nothing, I squeezed the doorknob flat and walked inside.

Susan shook violently at the sight of me. "S-stay back," she said, her aqua blue eyes widened. She held a cell phone in one hand and extended a taser with the other.

I surrendered with open palms, although nothing she, the police, or anyone else could do would harm me. "I can fix this. You're safe. I won't hurt you."

"Y-you...don't come any closer," she said, waving. Her curly brown hair bobbed back and forth. "The police are on the line."

Susan's tone sounded like she might bargain with me if I did what she said.

"Okay," I said. "I'll explain. Just hang up."

She laid her cell phone face up on the desk. "Emergency Number" was on its display, along with a red light. She ended the call. "Ten seconds before I redial."

No pressure.

Thinking quickly, I pulled down my black Raiders t-shirt with care, exposing my necklace – the source of my powers. The green prism sparkled in the track lighting. I had no idea how she would react. Blood rushed to my ears and my heart continued to beat double time. Either she believed me or thought I was nuts.

"This radioactive emerald gives me super strength," I said.

To demonstrate, I lifted the desk with one hand and set it back down. Made of hand-carved cherry wood, it had to weigh a couple hundred pounds or more.

She triggered the taser. The electrified projectiles flew toward my chest and bounced off, dropping to the carpet.

I forgot to mention that part. "Yeah, I'm invincible, too."

Susan dropped down into the black padded desk chair and cursed.

"We're not completely sure how they work." I put my hands into my pockets. "Rhapsody found them in Reject High before it exploded. She has one."

"*We?* You two had something to do with that?"

I nodded, pausing before outing the others. "All of us did." I shrugged. "Sasha and Selby, too. Our principal and science teacher went psycho. . .it's a long story."

Susan massaged her temples. She must have a stress headache, like the one forming behind my eyes. "You winged my door into the ocean, like a Frisbee."

How do you apologize for that type of destruction? "I'll pay for it somehow."

She sighed. "We shouldn't ever meet without backup. Andy insists that I carry a taser. But it didn't even work on you. I couldn't have even called a 10-13 without help."

The code "10-13" meant committing me to the seventh floor of North Hospital, the "mixed nut" aisle, as I like to call it. *I'll escape to a foreign country before I'll go there.*

My heart dropped. "I mean, yeah, I broke some stuff, but I'm not a killer."

She hesitated and slowly exhaled. Was she actually thinking about whether or not that was true? "I know, Jason, but when you lose control and become...*this...*"Her voice trailed off.

This? What does that mean? Superhuman or crazy? I rubbed the back of my throbbing head. "You don't sound like it."

As I moved a little closer Susan backed up and bumped into the ceiling-to-floor bookcase hard enough for her to act like it hurt.

Palms still facing outwards, I asked her again. "So, you're okay, right?"

She kept hesitating. Were my questions that hard to answer?

"I'm fine," she finally spat out. "I'm not counseling you anymore, that's for sure."

For the first time, I noticed she had pulled up the window and blinds and kicked out the screen. The air currents flowing through it cooled some of the moisture beading up on my forehead. "Alright," I said. "But you shouldn't tell anyone about this. Not even your husband. We have enemies."

The doorbell chimed twice. Thank God. My stepmom was early for once. Technically, Debra hadn't been my step-anything since my father divorced her nine months ago, but it was easier to call her that than something else.

I backed against the beige wall and leaned against the doorpost.

Susan's shoulders dropped and she relaxed her stance more the farther I moved away.

With nothing else to lose, I confessed to my therapist. "I just want to be...*normal.*"

Susan moved behind the desk. "We talked about this. The goal for you was psychological health, not a murky definition of normal."

Normal? Healthy? What's that even like? A tear escaped from my left eye though I tried stopping it. "You know everything now. Who's gonna help me if you don't?"

Susan's eyes watered. She wanted to do something, but I scared her. "As long as you're wearing that...thing... 'normal' isn't an option for you."

She had a point. Taking it off would mean I couldn't protect myself or anyone else. "I can't do that," I admitted. "Not yet."

I heard a gasp and a deep sigh behind me. Debra must have sensed Susan's discomfort. On her neatly-curled black hair she wore a navy blue headband that matched the color of her postal uniform pants. The shine on her dark complexion must mean the air conditioner in my aunt's van had leaked too much Freon again.

We exchanged glances for a second. From the look on her face and the way her lips twisted, I figured Debra knew the story. "What happened?" she asked.

I looked down at the taser projectiles in the dark blue carpet. "I chucked her door into the ocean," I mumbled.

"My God," she said. Debra, who was a little taller than I am, walked past me into the office. "Dr. Lin, are you alright?"

Susan shook her head. "I'll be fine, Ms. Brown. From a professional standpoint, I shouldn't have counseled Jason alone. That's on me."

Still sweating, I noticed my heartbeat had evened out. "She knows," I said.

Debra had looked relaxed up until that point. She buried her hand in her pocketbook for a check and flushed with embarrassment. I'd done property damage and other little things before, but she had never had to clean up something quite this big.

"It's not your fault my son is a superhuman," she said.

Feeling pretty crummy as they talked about me, I excused myself to Susan's office. After checking the area for bystanders, I stepped through the broken window and leaped down into the sand. The door hadn't gone far, so I kicked off my athletic shoes and socks and walked into the surf up to my knees, wetting the bottom of my shorts.

Under normal circumstances, a beach visit would have been a peaceful trip. Sasha, my girlfriend, might have thought it was romantic and enjoyed it, too. Since Reject High exploded and her friend, Asia, died, she had needed a lot of cheering up.

I returned to the building with the door and propped it against the wall. By the time I came back, the color had returned to Susan's face.

CHAPTER TWO

dinner costs too much

Debra's reaction to this failure would set the standard for future screw ups. Keeping the emerald around my neck meant it was only a matter of time before I broke something else.

Halfway down the wooden staircase she broke the silence.

"Dr. Lin is going to comp this session, which is a good thing. We're footing the bill for the door."

I glanced away at the blowing palm trees. No way could we afford it.

"God will provide. He always has," she said, sounding positive about it as we swung around to the next set of stairs. A seagull cawed in the distance.

I tried not to swear. "Did God make me like this on purpose?"

Debra's face drooped. She looked into my eyes. "There's nothing wrong with you, Jason."

Why was she so calm all of a sudden? "I threw a door into the Pacific," I said, jerking my hands at my sides. "I'm wearing a radioactive jewel and it's not killing me. There's something very wrong with me."

She sighed. "Look, I don't think Susan's going to drop you as a client. Even superheroes need people to talk to. She knows that more than anyone right now."

I'm not a superhero. I dragged my feet down the next step. "Thanks."

Debra stopped beside me. "Jason?"

Here comes the other shoe. I could almost hear her breathing. "Yeah?"

She bit her bottom lip. "Ray's downstairs."

I stopped in my tracks. Peeking over the banister into the parking lot, I saw my father's silver Cougar ZJ parked next to our busted up blue van. He walked back and forth between the vehicles, holding my brother in his arms and making silly noises.

"For real?" I asked in a squeaky voice. "Cool. I'll go around back and be out."

"Don't. I invited him to come. He wants to be in your life, Jason."

I controlled my breathing again to constructively release my anger. At least that's what Susan said it would do. Instead, the salty air burned my nostrils.

"He doesn't pay child support for me or anything else. Make him pay for the damages to Susan's office."

"If I do, are you going to explain to him how you did all of that?"

A lump formed in my throat. "Why does he care. . . now?"

"He was a terrible husband. He doesn't get a do-over on that one, not with me. Parenting is different. Like it or not, he'll always be your dad. It's how it works."

She was hiding something. "What aren't you telling me about all this?"

"Do something for me." She placed her hands on my shoulders. "He wants to take you and your brother out for supper. Go. Eat your brains out, and play nice."

I crossed my arms. "Only if it's Giovanni's. It's pizza buffet night."

"That's my boy." She smiled so hard her eyes narrowed. "Tuck your cape in."

Debra said that when she didn't want me using my powers. Easier said than done. "I'll work on it."

When we made it downstairs Zachary giggled and clapped over Ray's shoulder. We never spent much time together anymore, with me always looking over my shoulder.

"Ma-ma," Zachary said, stretching his chubby arms forward toward Debra.

Ray turned to face us. I tried not to look at his medium complexion, his forehead, or even the shape of his hairline, because I resembled him so much. Zachary lucked out and looked more like Debra.

"Hey, Champ! Deb, good to see you."

"Hi, Ray." Debra waved at the Cougar's tinted windshield. My other stepmother sat behind it. "Hey, Julia."

When I didn't greet my father, Debra twisted her mouth at me. I kicked a pile of loose parking lot gravel and nodded in his direction. He might think I was smiling, but I squinted at him because of the bright afternoon sun.

Ray pulled a white envelope from the right pocket of his gray silk dress pants. He passed it to Debra. "Here are those briefs I promised you. Look them over. I'm sure you'll be pleased with outcome."

"Thank you." She ran her hand through her hair. "I've gotta get back."

His eyebrows rose. "I thought the Post Office closed around now?"

Ray didn't try to sound like a snob, but he really sounded like a snob.

Debra didn't let it bother her. She dug through her pocketbook, I guessed for her work badge. At least once a week she misplaced it. "It does," she said, finally finding the badge and clipping it to her left breast pocket. "I traded off with a girl, but I have to help close up."

"Oh. How's it going over there?" He sounded interested.

"The hours are better, so I can be with the boys. It's nice not to be a late night zombie anymore." Debra toyed with her worn pocketbook strap. Fidgeting meant she wanted no parts of this conversation. "And the office? How's business?"

He smiled. "Better than ever. We're doing some overseas negotiations now, too."

This whole exchange was weird with not one snappy comment from either of them. Debra checked her watch. Ray pretended to get a text. Then they said something to each other at the same time and broke into laughter. What was I missing?

"Later," she said. I watched her round the van's front and get inside.

Ray clapped his hands together. "Julia's in the car, so it'll be the four of us for dinner. Bring Sasha Anderson along. We haven't seen her in a while."

My father pronounced my girlfriend's name like she was a famous supermodel or something. She was gorgeous with an athletic body, so he had it half right.

I scratched the side of my head. "There's a reason for that," I said to him while scrolling through my iPhone contacts.

"Yeah? What is it?"

He didn't need to know the truth. I stopped short of calling her depressed. "She's been . . . well, anyway, I'll ask."

He patted me on the shoulder. "Do it from the car. You can Skype her."

Ray put Zachary into his car seat.

When I opened the rear passenger side door a blast of pop music greeted me.

"Hey, Junior!" Julia turned down the song pumping through the speakers. She looked at me over her designer Hristoff sunglasses and pulled up her black sports bra. Her honey-blonde hair fell over her shoulders. "Coming with us?" she asked me.

I cringe every time she calls me that. My father always went by "Ray," our shared middle name. He disliked being called Jason. I hated the names Ray and Junior. *Why can't she say 'Jason'?* Nicknames bother me, though my friend Rhapsody has called me "Cap" so much it has grown on me.

"Hi, Julia. Yeah, I'm coming."

"Chinese, it is," she said. "We're getting takeout from the buffet near the house. The salmon rolls are legit."

"Nah, we're doing pizza at Giovanni's. It's buffet night. Ray said it's my pick. Zachary likes pizza better than Chinese, anyway."

Her tanned face tightened. It was hard to tell what made Julia so angry. She'd sweated her way through an exercise class and hadn't showered. I could tell from the aroma of sweat mixed with strong perfume. We'd be eating carbs for dinner, too.

When Ray got in to the black leather driver's seat, Julia let him have it. I don't know anything about Egyptian women, but when this one yelled her nose wrinkled and she sounded like a wailing violin. I played Texas Hold 'Em on the iPad in Julia's headrest while they argued.

"Time-out!" I made a "T" with my hands. "Can I Skype already?"

"Go ahead," Ray said. Annoyed, he shifted into reverse and backed out of the parking space. "Just get a salad or something, babe. We'll do vegan tomorrow."

Julia leaned over and patted him on the gut. "Try *all weekend.*"

Using Julia's iPad, I opened the Skype app and dialed Sasha. The wireless connection fizzled two or three times before connecting for good. Her laptop was set up in her bedroom. Sasha's Skype was always open so her dad could check on her while he was away, though she never mentioned if he actually did or not.

While I waited I scanned the people walking in and out of the boulevard's high-priced boutiques. Holding my breath, I hoped Sasha wasn't a sobbing mess.

On the fifth ring the screen opened up to her pink and white Hello Kitty bedroom. Sasha gave me a slight smile, though it was obvious she had been crying.

"Hey." She rubbed lotion into her palm and applied it to her dry face.

"Just finished with Susan. Hungry?"

She ran a pink brush through her hair. Then the screen froze, but I could still her Sasha's hoarse voice. "I could eat, I guess."

"In the Cougar. Fifteen?"

"See you."

I pressed the 'snooze' button and exhaled. Ray turned his body around at a stop light. "She's still torn up over her friend, huh?"

"Yeah." I changed the subject. "The Wi-Fi connection was awful."

"It's the solar storms," said Julia, as she frantically thumbed at her frozen iPhone display. "Started up again, and they're forecasting a big one next week."

Mr. Peters, my Earth Science teacher, had lectured my class about solar storms right before he tried to kill me the first time. Needless to say, I didn't remember any of what he said.

Ray turned onto the crowded highway and smacked the black leather steering wheel with his palm. "Should've known better than to take the 48," he said.

My phone went off. My friend Rhapsody sent me a blitz of texts. The first one read, *Still on the couch?*

Too fast for me to type a response, the next one came through. *Crack safe tont?* Weeks ago we sneaked into the rubble of Reject High and stole a safe from Welker's office. The thing could have traps in it. If it did and we opened it I wouldn't die, but she might.

The last one said, *Couldn't wait anymore. Just ghosted thru it.*

My mind went blank.

In addition to turning invisible, Rhapsody could pass her body through solid objects. Sasha called it 'quantum tunneling', but we nicknamed it "ghosting."

The last time Rhapsody tried it she almost lost her legs.

I typed back, "Not on the couch. What's in it?"

Zachary cooed and played with a teething toy. It sounded like an annoying, psychotic dog. Julia turned the music up so we didn't have to hear it.

Rhapsody didn't immediately respond. Had the thing blown up in her face, like I'd thought it might?

I leaned close to the window to see our whereabouts. We were at least forty-five minutes away in traffic. Crap! Thanks to the crystal, I had this incredible ability to leap into the air at tremendous speeds. I could get over to Rhapsody's house in no time. All I needed was an excuse to get out of the car. Diarrhea was lame, but Ray might buy it.

"Come over and find out," she finally messaged back, adding a winking smiley face.

What was in it? My patience broke. "Hey, Ray, can we pull over?"

"What's up, Junior?" Julia asked me. She must have heard me cursing under my breath after Rhapsody's text. "Problems in paradise?"

Trying not to roll my eyes, I looked down. "What does that mean?"

She giggled like a little girl. "You and Sasha, silly. Everything good?"

Ray hushed her. "That skeleton they found in the rubble of their school."

Julia's mouth dropped open. "Wha-?"

"The building exploded. Sasha's friend was killed. Sasha's hardly okay, babe."

Hand at her mouth, Julia gasped. "Oh, God! I'm sorry. Were they close, Junior?"

Sasha and Asia had eaten lunch together, and they'd gossiped by text. Beyond that, I didn't think they cared about each other at all. Sasha had been fine about it until last month, when the police had publicly confirmed Asia's identity. Since then things had become mega-weird between us. Today would be the first time I'd seen her in days.

"Yeah, they were close," I lied. "They went to middle school together."

Julia reached her left hand back and patted me on the forearm. "Just be there for her," she told me. "Listen to what she's not saying."

"Okay," I said, pretending to understand. The sounds of my little brother, who was gurgling and making raspberries next to me, made more sense than listening to nothing or to Julia.

Julia squeezed my hand close to the wrist. "You might want to dial back your friendship with Rhapsody, too. Just for now."

My head jerked back. What did she have to do with Sasha? I thought about it and still couldn't come up with a good answer.

Julia turned back around and boosted the radio's volume.

CHAPTER THREE

Ryan Cain, the magician knife-thrower

I entered the code for the black iron gates at Sasha's subdivision and waved at Nick, the security guard. Within minutes we arrived in front of the Anderson's house.

I checked my mouth using the face of my cell phone as a mirror. Nope, no drool. No new mustache hair, either, even though I'd skipped shaving for two whole weeks. I needed a haircut. My cheeks were puffy – had I actually gained a pound for once?

When we parked, I expected Sasha to lock up and strut toward us in a stylish outfit. She'd have her dark brown hair in a ponytail. Sasha's favorite wedge platforms made her a half-inch taller than I am. But to my surprise she didn't show.

We waited for a few minutes. Zachary played with his dog.

I pretended to be busy on the iPad while Julia talked to my father. "I like the stone accents, and it's the perfect shade of tan," she said, waving her index finger at the beige, two-story house. "But the angular design and the recessed front porch is so. . . sterile. Shame we didn't look at this neighborhood. I like the house next door."

"It's probably in the high nines," He chuckled. "Way too pricey for just us."

I gagged. Of course, he wouldn't think of his sons staying there.

"Three-car garage, Ray!" She elbowed him. "The backyard must be crazy."

Ignoring them, I got out of the Cougar and made my way up the multicolored stone walkway to the front door. Sasha had unlocked it. Her neighborhood was everything Ray said it was and more. No one with half a brain would break in here.

I heard a creaking sound in the floor upstairs.

Was that Sasha? I tried not to make much noise, just in case it was someone else. Stepping carefully across the eggshell white carpet without making a sound was harder than it sounds.

A board creaked underneath my sneakers. The adrenaline in my body must have kicked on my powers. Welker wouldn't be up there. He knew how to make an entrance.

Rhapsody and I didn't know our real enemy, but I didn't want to meet him like this.

I laid my hand on the lacquered banister. Didn't Sasha hear me?

Maybe she couldn't say so.

As I eased up the carpeted steps I heard a voice I recognized – Asia? "Hey girl," she said over a speaker-phone. "Too busy for your homegirl? Must be your new man."

Sasha sniffled. I moved another step closer to the top, stopping when the floor made noise. For a million dollar house, it sure wasn't a quiet one.

"Don't have to worry about me with this one. Straight arrows aren't my style."

I'm a straight arrow? Did she date convicted felons? I remembered Asia was dead because of us and I felt ashamed.

"Anyway, call me back." The line disconnected. Sasha sniffed, blew her nose, and replayed the message.

By the third time she did that I was in front of her white door. I knocked and pushed it open by the brass knob. Sasha sat on her bed, cell phone in hand. Her hair was loose and natural around her face, which had hints of red. She was still in her pajamas, a pair of pink Hello Kitty boy shorts and a matching tank top. Pretty, but sad. Tears flowed from her red-rimmed eyes and her shoulders trembled.

"Funeral . . .was. . .today," she said, her breath hitching in between her words. With her trembling hand she smoothed the Hello Kitty comforter on her bed.

No way am I sitting down this riled up. "What? Already?"

She turned her head toward the obituary propped against her darkened laptop screen. Written in script above her school picture were Asia's full name and two dates.

I mouthed the second one – May 17, the day Reject High exploded and killed her.

According to the news report, policemen identified Asia by an old break in her ankle bone. Sasha said Asia snapped it roller skating at her twelfth birthday party.

She sobbed a little, and then suddenly she stopped.

"Did you go?" I asked her. The room shrank a little.

". . . sort of," she said, almost collapsing again into a crying fit.

She'd used her powers and sent a clone? Had she done that with me, too?

I squinted my eyes. "Would've gone with you."

Sasha gave me a knowing glance. Funerals and I don't mix too well.

Without another word, I approached Sasha and lifted her into my arms. She curled against me like Zachary did when he was upset or tired. "So, they have this new, reduced-calorie white pizza at Giovanni's," I said, rocking her back and forth.

She dabbed a tissue at her running nose. Her eyes said she didn't believe me.

I squeezed her side. "You won't know for sure unless you come with us."

Sasha buried her face in my chest. "Give me a minute to put on a happy face."

A short time later Sasha came to the car, exactly like I'd thought she would. No strutting across the neatly-trimmed green lawn, just a simple walk. Her outfit didn't disappoint me, though. She wore a pair of white denim cut-offs, the off-the-shoulder Raiders shirt I bought her and a white tank top underneath. She'd gathered her curly hair into a ponytail and she wore her sandal cork-soled platforms.

Instead of opening the rear passenger door from the inside, I got out to meet her.

"Well played, Champ," Ray said. Julia added something positive I didn't hear.

Debra had taught me to be a gentleman during dates. Sasha liked it when I tried.

"Hey, Mr. and Mrs. Champion," she said to my parents. This version of Sasha was still upset, but closer to normal. "Thanks," she said to me.

"No worries," I said.

As soon as Sasha closed the door she started massaging my left hand. We rounded the cul-de-sac and left the high-class neighborhood. Passing rows of similar-looking expensive houses bored me. I laid my head against the leather headrest.

The next thing I knew we were pulling in to the downtown shopping center where Giovanni's is located. The clock on Ray's stereo said 6:15. I had fallen asleep on the drive. My session with Susan had ended just before five, and we must have hit rush hour traffic crossing town with Sasha. Not like Ray was in a hurry to get to this "hood pizza place."

The frigid air conditioning inside the restaurant helped wake me up. I'd memorized each piece of Oakland sports memorabilia hanging from the hunter green walls, dating back to the '70s. Sasha held Zachary, who had fallen asleep on the ride, too.

We stood in line behind Ray, who flashed his black American Express card to the cashier. Show off. He could've used debit, cash, or a card with a limit.

Julia made a beeline for the girls' bathroom, which had a pink Jim Plunkett jersey hanging from the door. She mumbled under her breath in what sounded like another language.

Ray poked me in the shoulder. "*Arabic*. Don't bother trying to understand."

I didn't get it or *her*. "Agreed," I said, patting my growling stomach.

Meanwhile, Sasha lingered with me at the counter near the cash register. She tapped her fingernails against the crumb-ridden white surface. If I'd had a scarlet emerald I might have tried to read her mind.

A slight smile curled from my girlfriend's lips as my little brother drooled a small spot on her t-shirt. "Remember last Sunday, when you gave this to me?"

I stopped inhaling the scent of mozzarella and sauce to look closer. Her chest was bigger than usual. Rhapsody crushed her in that department, so I think she wore push-up bras a lot to level the playing field. "They look great," I told her. "*It*, I mean."

She leaned in close, ignoring my mistake. "We should jump into the Coliseum for a game sometime."

I loved the Raiders, so the potential was there, especially if it cheered her up. But football season was still three months away. "Okay."

Ray wrapped up his purchase and we filled our drink cups at the soda dispenser. That's when Julia rejoined us. She'd tossed her hair up into a bun, put on some blush and a teal blue Nike warm up jacket. She seemed to be in a better mood when Ray handed her a cold bottle of Dasani water.

We all made our way to the buffet at the center of the restaurant's dark blue tiled floor. My stomach rumbled. Since the place was deserted, I loaded up on sausage slices.

Sasha held up a plain slice. Grease dripped from the stringy cheese dangling from the bottom of it. "Is this the low-cal version?"

"You know what? I think they're out," I joked while sipping my Sprite. "Blot away."

Julia might as well have been a rabbit with what she put on her plate, and Ray crammed his full with pasta in a creamy white sauce. It was a nice, peaceful outing. Normal is not my life anymore, so something ridiculous was bound to happen.

Then Rhapsody text messaged me again. Good, she was still alive.

I glanced at my phone's display. Sasha gave me a sideways glance and sucked her teeth. I didn't have to tell her who was texting me. She already knew.

She cut her eyes at me when I slid my fingers across the screen. "Tell her to chill. We're eating."

"Yeah," I mumbled while chewing. I switched it to silent mode. Powering down wasn't an option. Not after she'd opened the safe. Something might happen.

"How are your folks doing these days?" Ray asked Sasha.

She looked down and bit her lip. Sasha talked about her mom, Joyce, or her grandma. She never spoke about her father, who I finally found out was named Wesley. "Dad's on the road," Sasha said. "And Joyce," she shrugged, "is Joyce – working, as always."

While Wesley was always on the move, hiring talented executives for his company, whatever it was, Joyce had late dinners with clients.

I met her once. She did not say, "Hi," or "Nice to meet you." All she said was, "Let's not get ourselves put on the Internet, all right?" Sasha had cried on and off for about an hour, and nothing helped calm her down.

I stared at the framed and signed Ray Guy number eight jersey and trading card on the wall to my left. Ray and Julia talked in each other's ears and laughed. Zachary had woken up in time to smash small pizza bites onto his face.

"Going in for seconds," I told Sasha as I slid out of the booth. "Want anything?"

"I'm good," she replied, busily dotting grease away with a napkin.

While I scanned underneath the display glass for sausage pizza, I felt like I should check my phone. I dug it out of the right pocket of my shorts and scrolled through Rhapsody's texts.

Sasha stared at me from the other side of the buffet.

"What?"

She pointed her finger to the phone in my hand.

Oh. That. "Welker. The safe," I mouthed to her, waving my phone.

She blew me off.

I might as well read the texts now, since she was already annoyed at me.

Coming? The first one was stamped from a half-hour ago when I was asleep in the Cougar.

U with GG? "GG" was shorthand for "Girl Genius." Sasha swears that Rhapsody means it sarcastically, as if she is really a moron.

The last one said, "I found something." The time stamp was from a minute ago.

I replied, asking what she meant, and pocketed my phone.

That's when my body froze.

My ADHD kept anyone with a scarlet emerald from reading or controlling my mind, but they could stop me from moving. I searched around. Nobody moved, from the mounted Mark McGwire framed bat and glove at my far left all the way to the glass-encased football signed by Rich Gannon in front of me.

"Leave me a slice," a male voice said.

He was *behind* me. I recognized the voice – Ryan Cain, the kid whose jaw I'd broken last fall. *Who gave him a scarlet emerald and taught him how to mentally freeze people with it?*

He stepped in front of me, snatched the pizza off my plate and bit into it. About my size, he was dark-skinned and wiry, with a twisted braid haircut and a scarlet emerald chain around his neck.

I discovered I could talk. "You can chew? No more sucking through a straw?"

According to what I'd heard on Twitter during my suspension, he'd drank his meals for two weeks. It was a lucky punch, but it had served him right for what he'd said about my dead mother.

He continued munching. "Saw your family over there. Your new mom is hot."

Our fight had ruined Ryan's last chance with his latest set of foster parents, so they had sent him back into the system. From what I'd heard, they were nice, but even nice people have limits.

A few months ago, at my formal hearing, Debra had tried to make me apologize. "It might get you back into school," was her sales pitch. Like that would've ever worked.

And apologize for what? Being screwed up? Standing up for myself? Principal Rush, Mr. Tracy, and the lawyer didn't care what either of us did. They wanted us out.

Thinking about it made my head throb. *"Ryan started the fight. He admitted that. What was I supposed to do, get bullied until somebody noticed?"*

The lawyer swiveled in his padded cloth chair. Principal Rush smirked.

"All of you can piss off if you ever think I'll say sorry to him," was the last thing I said to them.

That had been my one-way ticket into Reject High.

Ryan wrapped his hand around the back of my neck, which was already hot. "Thinking about her right now? How much do you miss your *real mommy*, Junior?"

I cleared my mind before anger completely consumed it. It was the only way to keep from blasting Ryan through the ceiling. Once I could move again, that is. I wiggled my toes. *He's losing it*, I thought.

"You have something I need," he said, stressing the double-e's in "need."

"I'm not that kind of guy," I said. My leg muscles twitched with activity. "But if I'm gonna be your date, can I finish eating first? There's taco pizza coming out."

Ryan stuck me in the back with something solid – a knife? On instinct, I braced myself for pain. My powers had kicked in a while ago, so it didn't hurt.

I prayed for someone, anyone, to come in through the tinted glass door, but it was a slow night. *Isn't anyone around here wondering why I haven't moved in minutes?* I heard the workers laughing in the kitchen. This would have been a good time for Sasha to get up for more food, then she could help me. Not this time, though. My girlfriend eats like a slow moving pigeon, even when she's not depressed.

Ryan tried to snatch off my emerald necklace, but he fumbled with the clasp. Sasha and I had a jeweler set our prisms into titanium settings so they couldn't be removed as easily. Mine had a lobster catch, so it took concentration to unlock.

My tongue loosened. "I'm perfectly still, and you can't get a *necklace* off? You're going to be a virgin for the rest of your life."

Ryan waved his hand. From next to the pizza bar the utensil cups emptied. Steak knives rose into the air and pointed in the direction of our booth. Fortunately, I already controlled most of my upper body. I pretended to be unable to move my head.

"The provenance crystals," he growled. "You're going to help us."

So, not only did he know about me and my powers, he knew that provenance crystals grew the prisms. And "us" meant there was someone behind him pulling the strings. "Make me," I interrupted him.

Should've kept my mouth shut.

He nodded his head, and the knives zipped around the corner. A woman screamed in agony. It was either Sasha or Julia. Zachary wailed. Had he been hurt?

I seized Ryan's necklace and pushed my left palm into his chest. He rocketed through the air and crashed through the front door. Glass shattered and fell to the floor. The knives dropped. I hid his necklace in my shorts' pocket before anyone else saw it.

Sasha rushed around the corner. Nothing was sticking out of her body.

Julia?

The commotion alerted the workers. One of the Giovanni's girls came from the bathroom, spotted Julia, and fainted.

"Are you okay?" I asked Sasha. She'd seen a lot – exploding schools, fires, and her sometimes friend had burned to death.

"Julia," she said.

We scrambled over to the booth. Ray propped his wife up against the window. Three knives had plunged deep into the left side of her chest, right above her heart. Blood soaked her sports bra and workout jacket. It streamed over Ray's hands and dribbled across his knuckles onto the green padded booth seat. Julia's body started experiencing seizures and bumped against the table. Zachary giggled. He thought Julia was playing a game. Thank God at least he wasn't harmed.

Sasha took off her shirt and gave it to my father to help stop the flow of blood. Wooziness. I can't stand the sight of blood.

Zachary erupted with laughter, like he thought it all of this was a game.

Too much going on for me to think straight.

"Julia." Ray called her name over and over again. "Somebody call an ambulance."

Sasha ducked into an arcade driving game and duplicated herself. Clone Sasha rushed to the front of the store, where most of the employees were yelling and asking each other questions. I couldn't hear them over my heart pounding in my ears.

Ray cried. I'd seen him tear up only one other time in his life - when the pallbearers had lowered my mother into the ground. I didn't care for him, but Julia didn't deserve to die because of my mouth. She might make it to the hospital in an ambulance and live through surgery.

I didn't think so. Neither did Original Sasha, who pulled me aside and confirmed I already knew in my gut. "Do it," she said without hesitation. "North Hospital is fifteen miles away. I checked my traffic app. It'll take the ambulance too long.

"Ray."

My father ignored me. He tried to stop the pooling blood and keep Julia awake.

Kneeling in the booth seat against his, I called him again more loudly. "Ray!"

He shook his head at me. "We're not going to lose her. We'll get help."

Was he talking about Julia? It didn't sound like it.

I reached my right hand behind Julia's back and placed my left arm underneath her feet. From this angle it would have been hard for anyone else to lift her. But I picked her up like a stuffed animal, much to Ray's surprise. He'd never seen me do a pushup, much less lift a woman who outweighed me by twenty pounds.

Julia's voice drifted off. "Help. . . "

He stood in front of me. "Put her down! The ambulance will be here soon."

I shook my head. "She'll die. Open the door!"

Original Sasha dashed past my father and propped the back door open with her foot. "Go." She pointed to the parking lot. "I'll make sure no one else follows."

Holding Julia firmly, I jogged toward the rear of the building near the blue dumpsters. I'd have to even out my thoughts so we wouldn't travel too fast. I didn't need to check for the address of the hospital. I'd memorized it a long time ago.

Ray followed after me, pointing his bloody fingers and cursing.

How did he get past Sasha's clone?

"Get her back in there," he said. "I'll lock you away myself if she dies. Just wait."

I cursed back at him and turned in the general direction of the hospital. Large oak trees blocked my view of the town's skyline, but I thought my sense of direction was good.

At least I hoped so.

If we didn't hurry, we'd have an audience. Police sirens were closing in. Ray didn't need to see me jump, but I had no choice short of knocking him out cold.

Blood from Julia's wound soaked into my shirt near the white Raiders' emblem. Her eyes fluttered and rolled back into her head.

"She'll be your second dead wife if I don't do something," I said.

Shaking his fist, Ray continued shouting until I burst into the air and could no longer hear him.

CHAPTER FOUR

my first arrest

In a flash, we landed near the ER entrance. It wasn't dark yet, so we could have been seen, but I didn't notice anybody around. For the moment, things appeared to be all right.

Before I reached the automatic doors with Julia, two men in scrubs saw me carrying her limp body. They grabbed a gurney and wheeled it in our direction. Neither of them asked how I got there, which was a relief.

A third man escorted me over to the front desk. There, a short, Hispanic woman with a patterned hospital blouse stared me down. Julia's blood wet the front of my shirt. Thank God my clothes were dark colors. Otherwise, I would've looked like an amateur butcher or serial killer.

"Her name is Julia Champion," I said, pointing to the men rolling her away. "I'm her stepson. I don't know what insurance she has, but she's got it. She has money, too."

"Have a seat," said the woman. She pointed to the waiting area. "Wait over there, young man. We'll straighten it out."

Instead of doing what she said, I waited until she wasn't looking and practically ran for the bathroom. I tried not to vomit while cleaning up the blood. Carefully peeling off my shirt, I squeezed the extra liquid off of it. Then I used the paper towels and hand soap to wash up. I scrubbed my hands and fingernails last and reluctantly put my damp shirt back on over my semi-clean body. Afterward, I rinsed out the sink, which had temporarily turned bright pink.

Something inside me told me I should leave. Still, I wanted to wait for Sasha, so I returned to the lobby and dropped my body into a cushioned chair. The television was tuned to the Weather Channel. Mellow music played between segments where meteorologists talked about the solar storms raging across the world.

"X-class flares will steadily build in force across the surface until peaking next Friday," said a male voice. An animated display showed the yellow sun erupting with small explosions. "Best case scenario, sometimes your electronics will work. Worst case, at the storm's height, your cell phone will become a portable explosive."

"Wonderful," I said out loud. My cell phone had a full signal, but Rhapsody still hadn't messaged me back. *What's your 20?* I sent her in another text.

She did not answer. Maybe her service was down wherever she was. She could be visiting her dad. George was in a coma and cell signals in the ICU were horrible.

Sasha once said that she thought solar flares activate our prisms' power. *She's smarter than I am, but I'm not sure.* Could it be *that* simple? *And beryl is a gemstone.* Did that mean everyone wearing one as jewelry would become

like one of us? Or did they have to be from the source crystals?

Before I nodded off completely, she found me.

"Hey." Sasha joined me in the waiting area. Ray was impatiently filing out admission paperwork for Julia. "Maybe we should get out of here."

"Agreed. How is he?" I asked her as I eased out of my chair.

Her mouth tightened. "We left after you took off. He drove on sidewalks, back roads, whatever, to get here. He saw Clone Sasha. That didn't help *at all.*"

"How did you explain? Long lost adopted twin sister?"

"Hardly," she said. "He knows I'm an only child, remember?"

The only reason we were in this mess was because of Ryan. "I could kill him."

She rubbed my back. "Don't do that to yourself. You saved Julia. You did the same thing for Debra. She's on our side. Who's to say Ray won't be?"

"He promised to put me in jail if she dies," I said, exhaling loudly.

"Juvie," she corrected me. "Your birthday is still a month away, baby."

"Thanks." I didn't want to laugh, but a chuckle sneaked out. "He forgets my birthday on purpose. He probably thinks I'm already sixteen."

"Why would he do it on purpose?" Too late to stop her from asking, she realized the answer – it was three days after the anniversary of his first wife's death.

She laid her head on my shoulder. "I'm proud of you."

"For what?"

"Doing the right thing," she said, kissing me on the cheek. "Let's go."

We held hands and started for the exit. Reject High's former Student Resource Officer, Stu Spivey, met us there with a heavyset white woman beside him. She wore a blue dress shirt, black tie, and black slacks. The Giovanni's manager. Crap.

"That's him!" she shouted, pointing at me. "He stabbed that lady, Julia."

Dazed, I stood there and watched the scene unfold. Spivey gripped my forearm and pulled me toward his squad car.

"Resist," he said under his breath. "I dare you."

I wanted to take him up on that, but I played along.

Sasha piped up. "You know he didn't do. . ."

I hushed her. Now wasn't the time for Sasha to come to my defense, or for a show of super strength. "I've got this," I mouthed to her.

The manager stared at me as I got hauled away. God only knows what else she'd said besides that I'd attempted to kill my stepmother. Sasha, Ray, and anyone with two eyes knew exactly how Julia had gotten stabbed. I saved her life. I didn't try to take it.

Spivey handcuffed me and put me in the backseat. From inside the caged windows, I watched Ray motion to me not to talk. He still didn't get it. Nobody forces me to do anything I don't want to do.

I yanked at the metal cuffs, but they didn't give. Suddenly a streak of fire shot into my right leg around my knee. *Did he stab me? Why can't I breathe?* I shifted my wrists and the handcuffs nicked my skin. *What's on them? Is it a different kind of ice?* I couldn't tell.

Everything Ray said replayed in my mind. He never went to church, so he thought little of what God could do. That wasn't a surprise. He didn't think much of me, either. No shocker there. He'd put me in jail? *I don't think so.*

Good thing Debra decided letting me stay with him over the summer was a bad idea, after all. Otherwise, I might have thrown a chunk of his penthouse into the Pacific. I'd saved his wife's life. To thank me, the last thing he'd said was that he was right all along – *I'd grown up to become nothing.* A part of me had died inside when he said that.

Spivey had one of his men show me to an interrogation room. It was nothing like the cold, dingy space I'd thought it could be. It was a regular room, with white walls and no outside windows. It was hot. The brown table at the center had seen better days.

I wiggled in the seat cushion of my metal chair. *Where's Ray?* He couldn't have been that far behind us, and he'd broken all sorts of traffic laws to get to Julia. I gasped for breath and tasted blood in my mouth, so I spit it out on the carpet.

Spivey entered the room alone, without my father or someone else to play "good cop." He took off my handcuffs and I got a quick look at them. They had white stones all over them. White ice. *That's what it does – you*

can use goshenite to take away someone's powers. Mine
hadn't returned, so he must have more white ice nearby.

Spivey shoved the table to the side, propped his chair
close to mine and sat. Our knees almost touched, which
made me squirm. "Hand over the chain," he said,
making a "come here" motion with his hand.

"Turn my powers back on . . . and I will," I said,
blinking through the tears forming in my eyes. It stung to
breathe. I told him the truth. Normal human beings can't
bend titanium with their bare hands. "Where are the . . .
real policemen?"

He laughed and pulled out everything in my pockets
– my money, cell phone, Ryan's necklace, and my ring of
house keys – and set it onto the floor. *Is that even legal?*

"You blew up the school," he said, sitting back down.
"Thanks to you, I'm back on the street. Good thing I was
on duty tonight. I've got witnesses saying you stabbed
Julia Champion and enough red crystals to make them
say whatever I want them to say."

I'd done quite a few illegal things in the past month –
beating up Selby, breaking into Peters' house and Reject
High, bribing a janitor, destroying school property . . .
and this was the one I'd go down for? "Ryan stabbed
Julia. You know that?"

"With floating knives? Tell that story and I'll get you
committed." He scooted his chair closer and his left knee
bumped into my right one, sending shocks throughout
my leg. "Talk about the provenance crystals. Where did
you hide them? Let's start with the green."

He couldn't read my mind to find their locations. I
moved them once a week to keep the trail cold. I tried

shuffling my thoughts, just in case he got past my ADHD and tried to find out. That's when another officer showed Ray into the room.

"I'm Ray Champion – his . . . legal counsel." Ray gathered my things from the floor. "We're leaving. Unlock his handcuffs. You can't hold him without a charge, and he didn't stab my wife. I don't know who or what did it, but it wasn't my son."

"He can't leave yet. Not until he answers my questions," Spivey said.

Ray faced me. "We can't leave yet. Not until you answer his questions."

I cursed out loud. *What's the point of having a lawyer for a parent if he can't withstand a little mind control?* "What are your questions, Spivey?" I sighed, bracing myself.

"The crystals – including the gold one – where are they?"

When adults use ice, it eventually wears off. To stall him, I figured I'd wisecrack my way through this until the effects disappeared. Since he wanted information, he wasn't going to kill me. I wasn't sure he could do it, anyway, white ice or not.

"Until your gofer tried to kill Julia, I didn't know there was a gold source. Search your feelings. You'll find the truth, my son."

"You think that's funny? I'll throw you in a cell right now. Laugh all you want."

I hadn't been charged, photographed, or finger-printed. *Don't I get my rights read to me? Does anyone even know I was in here?* My breathing got easier all of a sudden. The pain in my knee faded. There was nothing Spivey or anyone else could do to stop me.

"C'mon, Ray," I said to my father, who was basically a well-dressed statue at this point. I stood. "He's not putting me anywhere."

Spivey drew his gun and aimed at my father's head. "Another move and he dies. Remember, you're not the one with the speed, Selby is."

I stepped in front of Ray and grabbed Spivey's right wrist. When he squeezed the trigger, a flash of heat surged from the fingertips of my hand to the rest of my body.

The bullet exploded from the chamber with a small trail of smoke behind it. The bronze-tipped slug slowed down in midair before pausing squarely in front of my face. I felt a pointy surface under Spivey's uniform sleeve. Red ice bracelet. Both Ray and Spivey stood frozen in time. After removing the bracelet, which also had white ice on it, I held it in my right hand.

I touched Ray's shoulder and he snapped to attention. Ducking down, he breathed heavily and frantically checked his body for holes. "What happened?"

Reaching out for the paralyzed bullet, I crushed it in my palm. Then I pushed Spivey into his chair and handcuffed his wrists behind his back. "You're in the police station," I said, taking Spivey's gun, cell phone, money, and the keys to open the cuffs. "Friendly neighborhood lawman here shot at you."

Ray rubbed his eyes and straightened up as I filled my pocket with Spivey's stuff. "This isn't happening, this isn't happening, this isn't happening... wait, are you crazy? You could be tried as an adult! Think about this."

"Okay." I paused for a second before backhanding Spivey across the face. "Thought about it. Now he's going to answer *my* questions." I looked Spivey in the eye. "It's been months. What are you waiting for? Why now? Why haven't you and Welker come after us?"

Ron Welker, his boss and my old principal, had powers, too. We had duked it out in the Reject High gymnasium and destroyed the school. He'd been missing ever since.

"King can't find the gold," he repeated it.

Ray scratched his head. "Stop it, Jason. Let him go now and I can plead you out."

I shushed Ray. *King can't find the gold? What does that even mean?* He wasn't making sense. "What 'King'? What does finding the gold source have to do with me?"

"You're the only one who can move them fast enough. We have a few days."

A few days? The solar storm? Next Friday, Sasha and I planned to picnic with my family at the park – so much for that. "Why? The storm..."

"Days until what?" Ray asked him. Spivey didn't answer.

I pressed the issue myself. "What if I don't?"

He had to answer my questions, as long as the red ice held power. Spivey writhed in his chair. "They'll explode – all of them. Nuclear bombs."

The apocalypse. I guess all those parents were right about me, after all. Sasha was on target about the solar flares and their effects on the crystals. If Joyce paid her daughter any attention, she'd send Sasha to a charter school. "Who's King, or 'the King'?"

Spivey muttered something I didn't understand before passing out.

Ray grabbed me by the forearm, but I snatched away. "Don't touch me," I said.

"Julia, she's..."

Before he could finish, I opened the door and stormed into the hallway. Ray got behind me and tried to catch up, but the hallway was too narrow for us to walk side-by-side.

I hustled past a trio of policemen and a pretty blonde with "Department of Homeland Security" stitched in white letters above her jacket pocket.

"Wait!" she shouted at me. "I need to talk to you."

Her name was on a badge hanging from her neck. I tried to read it without stopping, but she probably thought I was just starting at her boobs.

Once we were outside Ray keyed the alarm to the Cougar. When I got close to it, Sasha flung open the passenger side door. She hugged me and kissed me on the lips. My shirt was stuff with Julia's dried blood and I know I smelled awful.

I let go of her. "It's Spivey's," I said, showing her the cell phone. "We can use it."

Sasha snatched it from me and sprinted into the police station. My jaw dropped. "What's she doing?" I muttered.

Whenever Ray talked about women in front of me, he said they had at least four different agendas going on.

That doesn't include the one they allow us to know about.

My father cornered me next to his car. "There was a four-car accident on I-48," he blurted out. "If you hadn't. . . done what you did, Julia..."

"Forget it," I said, backing away from him. "Are we even now?"

His brow scrunched. "Parenting isn't a quid pro quo thing. You mean for your therapy? You don't owe me anything for that, son."

Breathless, Sasha returned to the Cougar before he could say anything else. "Take me to the roof?" she asked.

Other than to come over to her house so that we could hook up, my girlfriend never asked me to use my powers for no reason. "Go be with your wife, Ray."

"Jason, no. What the he..."

"Go," I interrupted him. "We'll get home safe. Debra already knows."

His eyes widened. "What do you mean 'she knows'? She's in on all of this?"

I shook my fists. "There's no time to explain."

"Make time," he said, pointing his finger at me. "I'm not leaving until you do."

Sasha took my hand and we walked to the back of the police precinct. Ray followed us there. There was a large blue dumpster at the back of the building. All three of us ducked two feet behind it.

I showed him my necklace. "Radioactive," I said.

The word radioactive made him back away. "You're serious?"

I pointed my thumb at myself. "I'm strong and invulnerable. I can jump. Sasha clones herself. Rhapsody can turn invisible. Now you know, too. We're leaving."

"Wait, Jason!" he whispered. Sasha already had her arms around my neck and I was cradling her bare legs in my arms. "I'm staying here. Let me help you."

"Why now?" I asked him. "You never stayed before!"

He looked down at the ground.

It was true. It was a low blow, but I'd gotten to him.

CHAPTER FIVE

I have a weakness, after all

I vaulted us onto the flat roof. If we stood we could be seen from a distance, so we lay flat on our backs, turned toward each other, and chatted face-to-face.

Sasha's eyes had sadness in them. "That was a pretty cruel thing to say to your dad, Jason."

I waved it off. "Yeah, well, when Wesley disowns you, come and talk to me."

"My parents are getting a divorce. My dad lives somewhere in Oregon. I haven't seen him in two years."

Since I had met Sasha she'd made it sound like her parents were still together. "What?"

"They've been separated since I was thirteen. His trips and Joyce's late dinners – have nothing to do with business. They're seeing other people or whatever."

"Why didn't you say something about this before?"

She bit her lip. "It still hurts to talk about it, Jason. My mom kicked him out, and I don't know why. I avoid her because I'm afraid she'll tell me."

"Sorry." Inside I felt a little guilty about lashing out at Ray. I scooted over to get a view of the parking lot. The Cougar backed out of its spot and drove off.

"I have a confession to make," she said. "I've been experimenting with my powers and studying different things."

I rolled back over to Sasha. "Different things like what?"

She handed me Spivey's phone. "Here, look at this."

"I don't get it. I thought you gave this back."

Sasha made an expression that she does whenever I miss something. "I took Spivey's original phone back to the precinct after I cloned it."

"Hold on, since when can you clone *things*?"

"Not just anything. If I don't know exactly how it works, it's worthless."

I stared at the lit screen. "So, this does everything Spivey's real phone does?"

She nodded. "For the most part. Kind of like Clone Sasha."

"Uh huh." I wondered about the limits of her powers. "What about money?"

Her face twisted. "Can't do that. It's complicated. . .the watermarks and all."

Sasha is a terrible liar, but I wouldn't call her on it. The only way we'd need her to counterfeit paper or coin money was if we were on the run from the law or something.

Spivey's phone connected with a call to a blocked number. Sasha answered it and muted the call so we could listen in on the conversation.

Spivey didn't greet anyone, but retold everything that had just happened – he'd detained me, and I'd escaped. He left out the part where I slapped and robbed him.

"What now?" Spivey asked his partner. "Don't we need him?"

The person's voice was disguised. "Dispose of the body," he said. "Get there first this time. We don't need your people asking questions."

The call dropped. Whose body was he talking about, Rhapsody's? He killed Selby's parents – is that what he meant by "this time"? I rolled over to the roof's edge and peeked over. Spivey hurried to his car, turned on the emergency lights, and sped off.

I turned my face to Sasha. "If I stop him, we'll never find out who he's. . ."

Sasha placed a hand against my chest. "I know, but I'm not the one who can fly."

Jump. "I don't know where he's going!" I panicked. "He'll see us landing."

Sasha grabbed hold of my hand. "Baby, we have to go, like yesterday."

We got to our feet. I held Sasha tight and jumped without thinking. We soared over large business buildings and residential neighborhoods. Whenever he turned I set down on a building or a house and jumped again in his direction. Once we hit the highway my comfort level skyrocketed. It was a straightaway. There was little on the side of the road I could accidentally kill.

Before I realized it we were in the Harleysville industrial district where my mother and George used to work. The area shut down years ago. We used to be the Motor City of the West until about ten years ago.

A minute before Spivey parked we landed softly in the alleyway. Landing was something I'd been working on since Rhapsody tucked and rolled on a rusty nail.

"Stay here." I pointed to a nearby dumpster. "Maybe inside it?"

She looked me up and down. "Sasha Nicole Anderson doesn't get in trash cans."

I didn't feel like arguing, so I rushed past her to the backdoor of the nearest warehouse and yanked it open. The screeching hinges meant there would be no element of surprise, so I stormed inside.

The stress dried out my mouth to the point that I imagined there was no spit in it. I'd been this nervous once before, and I hoped this time it wouldn't be because someone else I cared about was dead. At the risk of revealing our location, I lit up our path with my cell phone.

Sasha bumped into me from behind and dug her face into my back when she saw what was in front of us. I stared because I couldn't *stop* staring. By the way Sasha shuddered behind me she must have known who was lying face down on the ground.

The body was completely still and twisted – dead, for sure. I couldn't tell much else about it beyond that, a strange blue glow, and the hideous smell of body fluids.

Two other things, however, were clear. I was looking at the body of a girl who hadn't died too long ago. Maybe someone we went to school with? And it wasn't Rhapsody. I couldn't relax about it, though. We were still looking at a corpse.

"Freeze!" Spivey shouted and opened fire.

Turning my back to the gun blasts, I shielded Sasha. Bullets bounce off of me, but these didn't. These were fiery darts that sizzled against my skin. Spivey had found a way to make white ice bullets, and the pain was unbearable.

One after another, the shots penetrated my flesh. Struggling to breathe between my screams, I closed my arms around Sasha and pushed off, like a sprinter from his stance. We rocketed forward, punched a hole through the building's metal walls, and skidded down an access road into a ditch.

I rolled over onto my stomach and fell unconscious.

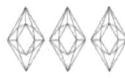

"C'mon, baby, wake up!"

Sasha must have been shaking me for a while, because she was out of breath and my neck hurt. As a matter of fact, *everything hurt.*

I slowly blinked my eyes. "Wha – "

"He's coming," she gasped. "We're not that far down the road."

I didn't remember how we got so muddy or why we were in a ditch. The answers to those questions would have to wait. My Adderall had worn off. Tonight I'd have to double up on the dosage or use the Concentra I pocketed from the doctor's office. *"They?"*

"Spivey, Welker, whoever." She grabbed my hands. "Get up."

When I moved my right knee buckled under my weight. It was hard to breathe, so I concentrated on short breaths. There was a stabbing pain in the middle of my spine. I slapped at it, but came nowhere close. Sasha hated it when I cursed, but it was torture.

She jumped behind me and dug her nails into the exact spot, which for a second burned like fire. "I missed that one. You had about fifteen of them in your back."

"Fifteen knives? Needles? Flaming steel spikes?"

Sasha pitched it into the open clearing behind us. "White ice," she said.

"They've made. . .weapons?" After I popped the Adderall pill I had stashed in my pocket into my mouth, my strength started returning little by little. Without the goshenite around my knee stopped throbbing. "Two minutes for the meds to kick in."

The flash of siren lights about a mile away grabbed our attention.

"We don't have that long," Sasha said.

Nothing surrounding us could provide us enough cover. Even at full strength, I'm a slow runner. With a flashlight and more goshenite, Spivey could easily take us down. My brain was all over the place. We could crash if I jumped us out now.

Sasha grabbed my hand and pulled me toward a nearby tree. Though its trunk was thick around, the two of us couldn't squeeze behind it. The rotted-out core couldn't fit one of us if we tried to squeeze into it. Climbing it seemed stupid, so I wondered where she was going with this.

"Get behind me," she whispered.

I did it.

Sasha touched the bark of the tree and closed her eyes.

Then something happened that I don't believe. Suddenly, where there had been one tree, now there were *four* around us. Then *eight*, more, and more, *dozens* – I didn't count them all. They'd just *appeared*. No glowing, sprouting up from the ground, or an earthquake. Each of them was an exact copy of the first, spaced out at a believable distance for a pop-up forest.

We had to split up – she chose the far end of the miracle forest, so I stayed closer to the front. *If something happens, I think I can stop it.*

Spivey sped right past us to the stop sign at the end of the road. He doubled back in our direction. He must have known the area well enough to realize it wasn't supposed to have so many trees.

Every time Spivey's flashlight shined in my direction I held my breath and stayed completely still. *How close does he have to be in order to try reading my mind?* Any thought would let him know I was nearby. In my mind's eye I pictured a black sheet of construction paper with no holes and tried to control my thoughts on that. It worked for thirty seconds. Then I wanted a loaded Pudgy Burger with seasoned fries.

Spivey laughed. "You're hungry, I get it. I'll buy you a burger. Come on out."

If Sasha had heard him she was probably cussing me out in her head. It's not my fault using my powers make me hungry. Ryan had interrupted my dinner, too.

"I've got goshenite rocks in this gun," he said. According to the sound of his voice, he'd be to my right, maybe a yard or two off. "Give up now, and I won't use them. I'm not trying to kill you, kid. We need your help."

You could've fooled me. I imagined telling him what he could do with his gun. I hoped my thoughts didn't get stronger the closer he came to me.

"Okay." He cocked the gun and readied to fire. "We'll do it your way."

One thing about a forest of identical trees in the dark – it's impossible to tell one from the other. By the time he actually found me my powers would be back to normal. *Just another minute. . .*

"Hey!" shouted Sasha.

How did she get here? I didn't see her. It could have been any of her clones. Spivey shot in her direction, but she disappeared into the darkness behind a fake tree.

"You missed," she said, taunting him from my right. He shot wildly, hitting nothing but trees and black air.

My strength finally evened out. Once I had his exact position I'd attack.

When Sasha appeared the next time she got a little too close and Spivey grabbed her. "You've got until three before I shoot," he said with the gun at her temple. "Three."

CHAPTER SIX

Sasha and I cross the line

I jumped forward, crashing through real trees and cloned ones to get to Spivey. I think his gun went off – I 'm not sure. Sasha couldn't be dead! Surely she'd managed to dive out of the way.

Once our momentum drove us to the ground I pinned the officer. Spivey spit in my face.

"What are you gonna do, kid? Kill me?" he asked.

He made a good point. If I let him go, all he'd do is come back after us. If not me, then Sasha, or Rhapsody, our families, other people. What was I supposed to do?

I wiped my forehead and sent a regular punch across his jaw. Then I dragged him by the ankles back to his patrol car, where his emergency lights still flashed. Susan had told me "stay in control." It took control not to knock his teeth out for spitting on me.

Sasha found me straddling Spivey's midsection, with my left hand at his throat. I must've squeezed the sides of his neck a little too hard because he started acting woozy.

"What are we supposed to do with him?" I asked her. "We can't let him go."

Sasha shrugged. "I don't know. You're going to kill him?"

I paused. "No, I guess not."

"Go 'head. . ." Spivey mumbled. "Kill. . .me."

Not really my style, but he shouldn't push me.

Sasha smacked my arm. "Wait, is that what you were thinking? We should *murder* him?"

I'd be lying if I said I hadn't thought about it. "Murder is definitely wrong."

"Right," she said halfheartedly. The red and blue lights flashed across her face. She was thinking. "We could keep him. . .*somewhere.*"

Who had time to watch a prisoner? "We can defend ourselves. What about our families? Wherever he goes he'll know who we are, everything about us."

Sasha's eyes brightened with an idea. "Not necessarily." She cloned herself. "Do you have any red isotopes on you?" Original Sasha asked me. Her mannerisms were sterile and cold. Clone Sasha, in the sundress she'd worn at Giovanni's, stood beside me and held onto my arm.

"Yeah, I do." I handed over Spivey's bracelet and Ryan's necklace. "Why? What do you need them for?"

She put a finger up to her lips. "Hold him down. I'm going into his mind."

Spivey wildly thrashed his arms and legs. "You don't have the nerve!" he screamed at her. "You don't have it in you!"

"You can do that?" I asked Original Sasha. "How? Can scarlet emeralds do that?"

She closed her eyes and concentrated for a minute. Sweat formed on her forehead. She gasped and put her hand to her mouth. Clone Sasha disappeared. Spivey stopped moving. The night was quiet, except for the soft clicking of the rotating red and blue police lights.

Sasha's lip quivered and she broke down. Crying bitterly, she walked over to me and planted her face into my chest. I held her tightly and gazed over at Officer Spivey long enough to confirm he was still breathing. His eyes were fixed on the sky and he blinked a lot. Whatever she did to him, it was *serious*. I said his name, "Spivey?"

He did not answer. His facial expression did not change a bit.

"Stu. . .Stuart? Can you hear me?"

Sasha's cries grew in intensity and she shook her head. Something had gone wrong when she went fishing around inside of his brain. Spivey *couldn't* answer me. Nothing good was going to come of our staying here with him.

I reached in Sasha's front pocket for Spivey's cloned cell phone and dialed 911. After giving the dispatcher his information and location, I hung up and gave the phone back to Sasha. She had quieted down, but her body was shaking. I placed Spivey in the driver's seat of his car, hoping whatever condition his mind was in, that he didn't remember anything about us.

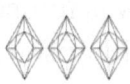

By the time we dropped down at Sasha's, it was after eleven. Joyce wasn't there – probably on one of her late night dinner dates. I wanted to go home and shower. I reeked of sweat and blood, and after tonight's events, I might actually sleep.

Sasha, however, was in no condition to be left alone. We usually relaxed for a while after weird nights – played video games or watched TV. It helped us feel like fifteen-year-olds without superhuman powers.

There would be none of that tonight –not after what I'd just witnessed. Accidently or not, Sasha had damaged a man's brain and turned him into a vegetable. The image of Spivey drooling on himself and staring into space etched into my thoughts. No one could pin us to it, but that didn't do anything for the guilt over my part in it.

We went upstairs to her bedroom. Sasha stripped down to her underwear and crawled underneath her pink and white bed sheets. She said nothing. I took off both my t-shirt and undershirt and got in next to her. Sasha faced me and lay across my chest. I stroked her wavy hair until the tears stopped rolling down her cheeks and she fell asleep. Soon my fatigue caught up with me and I felt myself drifting off.

Sometime in the middle of the night, my phone buzzed. I rubbed my eyes and scooted away from Sasha so that I could look at it without disturbing her. I'm sure Ray doesn't have my number, so it wasn't him. Was it Debra wondering where I was? She always expected me to check in, but tonight was unusual.

The text was from Rhapsody. The time stamp said 3:01 a.m. but the message section was blank. She could be in trouble and I had no way to find her.

I eased from beneath Sasha's arm and used my cell to find my way to her dresser. In the bottom drawer were supplies she stashed for me for times like this. I collected jeans shorts, an undershirt, Raiders t-shirt, underwear, lotion and a value-priced deodorant and sneaked into the bathroom connected to Sasha's room.

At the risk of waking her up or getting caught by Joyce, I showered and dressed as quickly as possible. It gave me a minute to wake up and think. Would she send me a blank message on purpose? Why would she do that? She can turn invisible, go anywhere. Where's one place she could go where I'd always find her, no matter what?

That's when it hit me. I knew where she was, or at least I thought I did.

I hated leaving Sasha. I kissed her gently on the cheek and pulled the covers up to her face. I transferred my things from my dirty shorts' pockets to the new shorts I wore. Tiptoeing downstairs, I got to the alarm keypad in the living room and reset it, allowing myself ninety seconds to get out of the house. As I entered the last number I sensed someone in the room. The end table lamp flicked on and I cursed.

Dressed in a shiny red bathrobe, Joyce lay back in a white leather chair, her legs crossed over the edge. Her eyes were bloodshot, and she held a drink in her right hand. The corked bottle wasn't far from her grasp. She swished the reddish brown liquid around and sipped it.

I froze, unsure what to do or say. For every second the alarm beeped, my heart beat two or three times. I waved, hoping Joyce didn't have a gun in her robe. I really couldn't handle being shot at again.

She tipped her glass and examined the contents. "So, you are. . . the boyfriend. . .or the *videographer?*" she slurred.

"Boyfriend," I said.

"The last one. . .he was both." Joyce let out a tiny belch. "Have a name. . . Boyfriend?"

The alarm kept beeping – I had, maybe thirty, forty-five seconds tops before it reset? Was she going to let me out? "Jason Champion."

"Jason Champion." She said it like my name was impressive. "Did you have fun?"

I pretended not to hear that. "Sorry?"

"I hear my husband likes blondes with legs. Do you like. . .blondes. . .*with legs?"*

Not blondes, really, but I did appreciate girls with nice legs. "No," I lied.

Joyce pointed her glass to the back door, which was a good fifty feet away. "If you leave here. . .my daughter. . .you come back to her. . ."

"Mom!" Sasha yelled from the staircase. Wearing a Hello Kitty bathrobe, she ran down the stairs and turned off the alarm just before it reset and locked me in.

"Sasha!" Joyce said merrily. "I was just telling the boy about some things."

Sasha took the liquor bottle to the kitchen, uncorked it, and emptied it out in the sink. When she finished she wrestled the glass from her mother's hand until it spilled. Joyce giggled and finished off what was left.

I met her in the kitchen. "I'm sorry."

"That's a. . .$200 bottle of brandy, young lady!" Joyce yelled at us, laughing.

Sasha refused to look at me. "Sorry for what, leaving me? Or my dad leaving me holding the vomit bucket and moving to Portland?"

Sadly, all of this was familiar. "I know how that feels."

She touched my right hand. "She's a joke. All her friends call her 'Corky' because she drinks too much," she said, trying to hold back tears. "I'll deal. Wherever you're going, *go*. She'll cuss me out in the morning for pouring out her top shelf brandy again and she'll forget you were even here."

"Are you sure?" I asked. "I'll stay."

Sasha held her hands to her mouth and let a sniffle escape. "Truth? We'd be upstairs asleep if you were going to stay."

It wasn't a fight I was going to win. I kissed her on the cheek and exited through the back door. Her intruder spotlight shined in my eyes. I walked out of its range and jumped away.

From the sky I could see that the area around Reject High was pitch black. It made sense that Rhapsody would try to meet me here. It's where we first met. Until I landed, I'd have to trust my instincts were right and I'd be in the right spot.

Sure enough, when my feet hit the pavement I was at the front door. The building had been stripped of everything important, including the security system. The place was a wreck. According to the news, the heating and air conditioning units had exploded because of a gas leak, not six super-humans fighting each other.

I felt around for the door handle and pulled it open. My cell phone cast enough light for me to see a couple of feet ahead.

I leaned against the wall and waited near where the metal detectors would have been. I sniffed the air for

Rhapsody's perfume and tried not to cough when I inhaled dust instead. *Was I wrong? Maybe she meant the gym – I saved her there. Or the cafeteria, that's where she kissed me. It couldn't be the dungeon, in its condition.*

The light to my cell phone dropped out. Right when I positioned my index finger to restart it, a hand gently covered mine and squeezed.

"Don't bother," Rhapsody said. "I'm here."

CHAPTER SEVEN

we make a plan

Without lights I couldn't tell if Rhapsody was visible again or not. She hugged me and held on longer than usual, even for my best friend, but it wasn't weird. I squeezed her back. The dust made me cough, which was a good excuse for both of us to let go.

"We're not safe – especially not *here*." Wiggling my fingers, I felt the grit in the air. It was like airborne sand.

"Like we're safe *anywhere*?"

She had a point. Now what?

"I've got a guy on the outside," she said. "He'll signal us if something's up."

A guy? My chest tightened. "Unless he's like us, it's not going to matter."

She paused. He was like us? Selby?

Rhapsody stopped short of answering me. She shined her cell phone's flashlight application onto her face. Without makeup, she looked tired around the eyes. "Somebody was mind-controlling him for a minute. He's not sure who."

Of course he's not. "I don't buy that crap. Why do you?"

"He looked out for me in elementary school. I needed help. Want me not to call other dudes for the job? Stop feeling up Girl Genius long enough to answer your phone. Quit blowing me off!"

"Fine!" I said, kicking at a loose piece of linoleum. "What's the big emergency, anyway? What was in Welker's safe?"

"Not yet." She keyed a text message on her phone. "We came to Reject High so you could find us. Staying anywhere too long will make us targets."

As soon as she pressed "send," Selby *whooshed* into the lobby and sent a violent rush of air our way. I closed my eyes and mouth. Rhapsody ghosted and it passed through her. When the breeze faded away, I saw nothing but his silhouette. When I swung at it on instinct he easily dodged my punch.

"Good seeing you, too, Freak," he said. "She told you about the. . ."

"Yeah, yeah," I said. "Mind control, *blah blah blah*. Tell it to my collapsed lung."

"Meet you at the rendezvous point," he said before zipping away.

Rendezvous point? Who talks like that?

"He's way too into this," I said out loud by mistake. "Where's this 'rendezvous point'?"

Rhapsody laughed a bit. "He's extra. Dude, it's just the old playground."

I knew which one she meant – the one where Selby had pushed her to ghost for the first time and she'd almost lost her legs trying to do it.

No one was going to get maimed tonight, I hoped.

Once we got outside I held Rhapsody's waist while we jumped to the playground. Its dull overhead orange lights allowed us to see each other. Selby, wearing one of his white practice jerseys and black shorts, relaxed on one of the benches. We joined him. It felt like an incomplete meeting without Sasha, but she had "Corky" to deal with.

Rhapsody pulled a small journal from the bottom zipper pocket of her black utility vest and handed it to me. "Read."

As I flipped the yellowed pages they made a crackling sound like dry leaves. Each had a bunch of penned drawings and equations on them, written in English, I think, but with symbols I didn't understand. "Carrington" was scribbled over and over again in black cursive.

Nearing the back of the journal, I saw the writings concluded with drawings of crystals and observations. Nothing was written next to "morganite," which were the pink stones, "heliodor," the gold, or "aquamarine," the blue.

Had the owner of this journal never figured them out? Or he didn't want anyone else to know what he did?

Selby must have seen confusion on my face. Sitting on the other side of Rhapsody, he leaned his head forward. "A scientific journal," he said. "At least, that's what we think."

Rhapsody reached over and turned the pages back as it sat in my lap). Her fingers grazed my leg and my heart jumped. "I Google searched for details on Carrington," she said. "It was a solar storm in 1859 – the biggest one in five hundred years."

I connected the dots – the book was *really old*. "Bigger storm than next week?"

"Nope," Selby jumped in. "Way smaller. Don't you watch TV, or is it just movies for you? It's been all over the news."

Most of the movies I saw were because Debra couldn't afford cable until we moved in with Aunt Dee. "King needs me to find the heliodor because I can lift it for him and move it fast."

Selby passed me an old photograph. "Heely-o-what?"

"That's what they call the gold crystal," I explained, taking the picture from him.

"Oh, well, maybe King is one of those people."

I stared at the picture of men in white lab coats and women in nineteenth-century formal dresses. The background was blurry, but it almost looked like a castle. "How would King still be alive if he was in *this picture* Selby?"

"Well, whatever," Selby said, taking the picture back. "Rhapsody found it in Welker's safe. I don't know, Freshman. Couldn't he be tracking down their relatives?"

She told Selby what she found before she told me? I rubbed the back of my neck and delivered the worst part of the news.

"He also said the provenance crystals are going to explode next week."

Both of them cursed at me.

"What? Like we're all gonna *die?*" Rhapsody asked.

"They're not anywhere close to here," I said. "At least not three of them."

Selby held his hands out. "You know where they are! So, we're good if we just stay in town?"

I might have been wrong for taking a second to think about it, but I did. Shaking myself I said, "I don't know, Selby. These things are like nuclear bombs. We might be okay. We might not. But a whole lot of other people will die if we don't do anything about it."

"If Spivey's telling the truth. Let me ask him. I'll get the truth out of him."

My shoulders tensed. Spivey was in no condition to be questioned, thanks to Sasha. "What good would that do? Are you going to run around him until he talks?"

Rhapsody rubbed my left hand, which helped calm me down. "Cap knows where the red, green, and white ones are. The other three could be in town, for all we know."

We all stood. I admit that I don't like anything about Selby, but running was a punk move, even for him. "You'd let innocent people die if you could stop it?" I asked him.

"You can't even drive. What makes you think you or anyone else can keep them from blowing up? Bury them underneath a jail. Those people aren't innocent."

Thousands of people would die if we stayed out of it. I shook off the cold shiver traveling up my spine. "I'll get the crystals together and hand them over. King, Welker, whoever – they could have a plan to stop them from exploding."

"Jason, think for a second," Rhapsody said. "Look at what we can do with three of them. You'd be giving them all six without knowing what they all do or what those people plan to do with them."

I backed away from her. What else could we do? The crystals couldn't be destroyed. When we'd tried smashing the green emerald it had blasted me unconscious.

"Move the red, green, and white," Selby suggested. "I'll help do whatever until Saturday. After that, I'm in the wind, and if you're smart, you will be, too."

He zoomed off, leaving a cloud of uprooted grass behind. The metal basketball net rattled in the distance.

I slumped down in the bench and dropped my face into my hands.

Rhapsody sat next to me and rubbed her hand across my back. "Do you really think they'd leave us alone? Or is that what you're hoping would happen?"

"No idea." My voice muffled in my hands. "I almost agree with Selby. We should just leave. Go north to Xobai County for a couple of days, live it up while we still can."

The perk in Rhapsody's voice dropped. I could, but she couldn't.

"Ruby's pulling the plug on Pápa. She told me to say goodbye. Our priest already gave him last rites."

I straightened up. "What? *Why?* She doesn't believe in that, does she?"

She licked her bare lips. "The insurance company believes in it. We've done it all – bike rides, beef and beers, highway donations. He's been sick forever, Jason. This is it. He's gonna die, and there's nothing any of us can do about it."

My heart broke for her. Losing a parent was the worst. I put my arm around her shoulders. We didn't speak. She cried for a long time. I wondered if she'd ever stop. Every time she slowed down, she picked back up again.

"I'll bring him green prisms every day until the storm."

Sniffling, she looked at me with tears still streaking down her tanned face. "You mean it? You'd do that for me? What about the explosion?"

"Screw it," I said. "We'll figure something out."

Rhapsody gave me a kiss on the cheek. I smiled. She smiled back. She gave me another peck, slower this time and closer to the corner of my lips. The scent of her perfume overpowered everything else around. I swore it was the same kind my mom used to wear.

I know where this was going. Shouldn't I stop it? She needs this. But. . .

The next time she kissed me, it was full and on the mouth. I hesitated at first, but then I kissed her back. She shed her vest and tossed it over the back of the bench. I wrapped my arms around her sides. We continued kissing. Her mouth tasted like cigarettes.

What's happening? We'd done this before, but not like this. I didn't feel the small chill in the air anymore, and I started sweating under my arms.

Suddenly, Rhapsody pulled away. "Sorry, Cap," she sniffled, putting her hand to her mouth. "I'm emotional, stressed out, whatever. Text it."

She triggered her powers and vanished before I could say anything. Thinking about returning to Sasha's to check on her, I wiped off my mouth, in case Rhapsody was wearing lip gloss. I took a self-photo on my cell phone to double-check.

After making sure no one was lurking around I left for Sasha's house. I touched down on one of the less steep parts of the roof near her room. The entire house was dark, except for her nightlight. I lightly tapped my fingers on her window. A minute later she dragged herself to the sill and waved – not that I should come in, but that it was too late for me to sleepover and I should go home.

I leaped to Aunt Dee's and used my key sensor to turn off the alarm from the backyard. The intruder light flashed on when I got to the gray cement steps at the rear door. Beyond that was an annoying door alarm hanging on the inside doorknob. When I went out Debra always deactivated that one for me. Otherwise, I'd wake up everyone.

Aunt Dee had a shotgun and she was trigger happy.

When I got into the kitchen I saw Debra leaning over an empty pot of coffee on the counter. She'd been waiting for a while.

Everything else but the sink was covered in plastic tarp. Aunt Dee had insisted we renovate the kitchen this summer, and since she'd taken us in and didn't have the money to hire anyone, she and Debra forced me to help.

"Morning, Cap," she said, scratching her black headscarf. "Breakfast?"

I checked the time on my phone. 4:45 a.m. "Yeah. Thanks."

Debra cracked eggs forever and laid an entire slab of turkey bacon into the pan. I watched her until my eyes drifted closed. After however long she took, I jerked awake with a full plate in front of me – scrambled eggs and cheese, turkey bacon, toast, grits, cereal and milk, with a mug of coffee. It smelled like a restaurant in the kitchen. I ate it all with no problem and scraped my plate clean.

My stepmom took my plate and washed it in the sink. "Busy night?"

"You could say that," I said, sipping my drink.

"After Dee got Zachary and you left the police station, Ray called me. He went on and on about floating knives, you flying, and Julia. . ."

I quickly swallowed the coffee in my mouth before I choked on it. "She's alive?"

"Yes," she said. "She's in North Hospital. You saved her life."

The next sip of coffee was a little sweeter than the last one. "You don't say!"

She lowered her voice at the sound of Aunt Dee walking across the floorboards upstairs. "A woman from Homeland Security came here looking for you."

My eyes widened. Homeland Security? "What's her name?"

"I don't remember," she whispered. Both of us heard my aunt approaching. "She left her card – I hid it upstairs. She said that. . ."

"Shh," I said. Aunt Dee was close.

"Just be careful," she warned.

Aunt Dee padded into the kitchen. Her hair was in rollers and she was wearing a purple nightgown with no bra on. I quickly chose something else to look at.

"Morning," she said. "What are ya'll doing up at 5 a.m.?"

I tapped my fingers against the table. "Couldn't sleep," I said. It was the truth.

"Deidra Lee, where is your bathrobe?" Debra asked her. "I just washed it."

Aunt Dee folded her arms across her chest. "That's why I can't find it, Debra Brown. Look at me, Boy. You miss your curfew? What time did you get in?"

"It's the summer, Dee." Debra waved her hand. "He was in the bed by. . ."

"Eleven," I confessed. "Woke up around three and never went back to sleep. Walked right past you. You were asleep in your chair."

Aunt Dee seemed satisfied with my answers. Half of them were true. She always fell asleep in her chair. She left the room in search of her bathrobe.

Debra and I smiled at each other. Finally, *someone* was on my side.

CHAPTER EIGHT

meeting a secret agent

I woke up in Aunt Dee's home office. She'd moved enough of her junk around for me to sleep on the day bed and to store a small amount of clothes. This was my room.

"Thank you, Lord, for this day," I kissed the framed picture of me and my mom. With that, I rolled out of bed and headed for the bathroom at the end of the hall.

While showering I flashed back to everything that happened last night. I'd made out with my best friend. My girlfriend had brain damaged a police officer. I'd learned the provenance crystals are going to explode in a week. Everything was all out of control.

Once I threw on a white Raiders t-shirt and a pair of black shorts, I thought about leaving the house from the roof, but anyone could see me. Debra always reminded me to be careful. Instead, I took the staircase and headed for the backyard. I passed Aunt Dee, who was feeding Zachary in the kitchen. I served myself some orange juice and took my Adderall pill, making sure to stash some extras in my pocket, just in case.

"Afternoon," she said. Thankfully, she had put on a pair of red sweatpants, a tank top, and a bra. "Hate how ya'll teenagers stay up so late and sleep half the day away in summer. We're painting the cabinets today, remember?"

I finished sending a text message to Sasha. "Hi, Auntie," I kissed her on the cheek. Zachary continued munching on the green paste in his mouth. I waved at him. "Hey, lil' bro. I'll be back in a little bit."

The news played on the TV, which half distracted my aunt. She played the lottery and would not miss the numbers being called for anything. "Uh uh. Clean up the room first and make the bed."

I knew she'd say that. "Yes ma'am, I did that already."

"You need to stick around so we can po. . ." Aunt Dee stopped talking when photos of Spivey and Julia flashed on the TV screen. "Lord Jesus! Debra!" she shouted.

Crap. I should've changed the channel when I had the chance.

"Police are investigating the disappearance of local police officer Stuart Spivey," said the anchorwoman. "Officer Spivey was last seen around 7 p.m. Thursday at a Harleysville restaurant, apprehending a suspect. The suspect was allegedly connected with the stabbing of twenty-seven-year-old Julia Mosri-Champion, wife of prominent Harleysville attorney Ray Champion."

Aunt Dee placed a hand at her heart and turned up the TV's volume. I looked away, but I felt her eyes burning holes on the side of my face.

We listened to the rest of the report.

"Mosri-Champion is in stable condition. The suspect was released and police have no leads as to Ms.

Champion's assailant or Officer Spivey's current whereabouts."

Debra appeared in the doorway, rubbing her eyes and yawning. She must have called in to work last night. I didn't know she had any days left.

"What's the big commotion?" she asked.

"Whoever stabbed Julia got this officer, too? Did you see it, Jason? Who's the suspect?"

"Deidra Lee," Debra said, laying a hand on my shoulder. "Let him visit his stepmother and stop asking so many questions. Whatever he knows, the police know."

Aunt Dee's face softened. "Sorry, Nephew. Don't pay no attention to your ol' auntie. You need a ride to the hospital? I'll throw on some better clothes."

I patted my empty right shorts' pocket. "I've got a bus pass. See you later."

I left. Debra watched me, silently mouthing "be careful" before shutting and locking the back door behind me.

I nodded and went straight to the basement's above ground doors. Unlocking them, I carefully walked down the steps. Behind some of Grandma Barbara's old dusty mementos was my stash of scarlet emerald, green emerald, and goshenite prisms. I grabbed the entire bag of green emeralds and surfaced.

As I walked out of the back gate I wondered where I should go first. I checked my cell phone – Sasha hadn't answered me and it had been fifteen minutes. It went straight to voicemail when I called. Nobody answered the house phone, either. Going over there meant talking about last night, which I definitely did not want to do. *She'll call me when she's ready, I guess.*

I dialed Rhapsody's cell and she answered on the first ring. "Hey."

"Hey," I said. "Headed your way in a sec."

"See you." Her voice sounded flat. Was she still upset about last night?

As I got to the overgrown oak tree in the backyard, a rusted, black late model van parked at the curb. Two people got out of the sliding passenger side doors – a tall, bald black man and a woman with dark hair bundled into a ponytail. Both of them wore dark suits and white shirts, no ties. What did they want?

"Jason Champion!" yelled the man. He waved something gold in his hand – a badge? Heliodor rock?

The two of them walked towards me, but hesitantly, like they knew what I could do to them. "We're from the DHS," she said with a heavy Asian accent.

DHS – Department of Homeland Security? And I had a hundred nuclear weapons in my hand.

I focused my thinking past my racing heart. They could be with Welker or King. Either way, I didn't think they were trying to help me.

And if I was in this kind of trouble, so were Rhapsody and Sasha – even Selby.

I took off for Rhapsody's house, soaring faster than I meant to go.

Slowing down on the downward arc was too hard, but I tried. When I landed the ground shook. Rhapsody looked up from the broken steps of her back porch. She wore a pair of blue cut-off denim shorts with black spandex beneath them and a white golf shirt. Her hair, dyed black everywhere but the roots, hung down past her shoulders. She was dressed to see her dying dad, George, who hated it when she looked Gothic.

We weren't alone.

Ruby, who was with her, did the Catholic cross thing over her chest when she saw me. She held the white gold crucifix hanging around her neck, looked at us and prayed, saying a whole lot of words in Spanish I didn't understand besides "¡Dios mío."

The blonde from the police station stood next to them. Like the other two at Aunt Dee's house, she wore a black suit with no tie. Up close, she was prettier than I first thought. She had a pointy nose and a nice figure, but that didn't change the fact that she'd busted us.

Rhapsody could have easily escaped. Why hadn't she?

The blonde has white ice and knows how to use it. For some reason, though, she wasn't using it on me. I could still breathe and my knee was holding up.

"Are you going to play nice, Jason?" she asked me.

A large, silver box the size of a guitar case lay next to her foot. What was in it?

I jammed the bag of prisms into my back pocket and held up my hands in surrender. "It's not like I have a choice."

"You always have a choice," she said, touching a tiny bluetooth headset in her ear canal. "I've got them," she said after a second or two. "Meet me at this location when you finish with Sasha."

Finish with Sasha? My insides boiled with anger. What did that mean?

The woman lifted the case by the handle. "After you, Ms. Martinez."

Ruby, dressed in her restaurant manager's outfit of black pants and a red shirt, led us. It was the first time I had been inside of Rhapsody's house past the living room in the front. The decorations were modest throughout and the white appliances looked yellow. I'm sure they weren't dirty – it was probably from age and use.

We passed Rhapsody's room. I expected the walls to be painted black and covered with some heavy metal posters or something. Instead, the room was white. Her bed had a tan comforter on it, and the carpet was a dull shade of brown. Spread out on the floor was a jewelry-making kit – necklaces and ring settings for the prisms.

Hidden in the far corner underneath a bed sheet was the safe we stole from Welker. The blonde paused in front of us. She noticed it, smiled, and moved forward. Curious, I took a peek myself.

"Quit it!" Rhapsody said, poking me in the back. "Eyes ahead. Keep going."

Her mom showed us to the living room, where we sat in off-white furniture pieces patterned with flowers. The DHS agent took the biggest chair. Rhapsody and I sat next to each other on the loveseat.

I put most of my weight on my left butt cheek, since the prisms were tucked inside of my right back pocket. Rhapsody reached over and held my hand to keep me from moving around so much. My neck got hot when she did that, so I let go of her fingers and made a fist. Ruby stood in the middle of the room and avoided eye contact.

"I guess I'll start," said the agent. She rubbed her hands against her gray slacks. "My name is Courtney Stafford and you should think of me as a friend."

"Why should we be friends with a Department of Homeland Security agent? Immigration, IRS. . .these are not friendly agencies to me." Ruby posed a good question.

Courtney sighed and eyed both of us. "We are your friends. Hear me out."

Ruby excused herself to the bathroom down the hall. Our "friend" lowered her voice to just above a whisper.

"Honestly, I'm not really from the DHS, but you need to know. . ."

"You showed me a *fake badge?*" Ruby shouted. "That's it. I'm calling the cops, like I should have done in the first place."

I threw up my hands. Rhapsody cursed and Ruby gave her daughter a look.

"Really with the staring?" she asked her. "Whoever-she-is from wherever lied about her identity! She's sitting in our living room and you're mad I said 'sh. . .'"

Ruby opened the front door. "Get out of my house, Lady, right now."

"Wait, Ruby!" I said. "She might know. . .about us. Who are you *really?*"

"That's actually kind of. . .tough to explain," she answered.

"Really?" Rhapsody said with all the sarcasm in the world. "Hi," she said, extending her hand to me. "I'm Rhapsody Lowe. Who are you?"

"Jason Champion." I played along, but didn't shake her hand. Things were still weird between us. "Not real complicated to me, *Courtney*. What do you think, Ruby?"

She waved her hand at her throat. Ruby wanted no parts of this conversation.

Courtney pursed her lips. "My real first name is Eris. Stafford is my last name. Call me 'Eris' *just once*, Jason, and I'll shoot you with goshenite in your good knee."

I doubted that. "How much do you know?" I asked with immediate regret. I wanted her to say next to nothing, but that's not the way my luck works.

"*Everything*. Including what really happened at Giovanni's last night and what you plan to do with those isotopes in your pocket."

The answer shut me and Rhapsody down. We were at Courtney's mercy.

"Can I get something to drink?" Courtney rubbed the back of her neck.

Ruby tapped her wristwatch. "I'm late for my afternoon shift." She held an open red flip phone in her hand. "You need to go, whoever you are. Now."

Courtney reached into her pocket and retrieved a white envelope. "Tell you what," she said, pointing to the kitchen. "Two year's worth of salary and an open ticket to Panama are in here. Give me a cold glass of water and ten minutes with these kids. If you still disagree with me after that, I'll leave and you can keep it all."

Ruby took the bribe and hurried to the kitchen.

Neither of us thought it was for the money or the ticket. She was afraid for us and whatever kind of trouble we'd gotten ourselves into.

Courtney scooted to the edge of the chair. "There's this story in the Bible where Jesus puts out everyone in the room to perform a healing. You know that one?"

I slept through church practically every Sunday, so I had no idea what she was talking about. "Uh huh," I said. "Jesus. Right."

Rhapsody playfully punched me in the arm. "We read that in mass. He kicked out everyone who doubted. What's your point?"

She licked her lips. "'DHS' means don't ask. That's why we say it. Some questions can't be answered. Others you won't want the answer to. Same kind of deal with us. We're not terrorists or government. Think of us as a utilitarian collective."

I could have used Sasha to translate *utilitarian collective*. I thought I understood. "A collective," I repeated.

Courtney synced a video she'd stored on her large screen smartphone and showed it to us. "You got on our radar last May, when you did this. We weren't sure it was anything unusual until Reject High exploded six days later."

They called it Reject High, too? Rhapsody huddled close to me to watch the video. I tried to move away but couldn't.

The screen played a looping flash of an object streaking through the blue sky. It was an amateur recording of my first jump.

Courtney flipped to a blurry photograph that had been blown up. In it a small part of my face was visible.

CHAPTER NINE

we almost get busted

Courtney knew about our powers, or at least *mine.*

"We cleaned up the mess at Giovanni's so that no one suspected you." Courtney folded her hands on her lap. "Brainwashing isn't as easy as you may think."

How many others knew? My stomach tightened. Rhapsody and I kept quiet.

Ruby, who poured the world's slowest glass of water, didn't say anything above a whisper from the kitchen. Was she praying? *Does she plan to hop the back fence and run off to Panama?* I swore the back door hadn't opened, but I could have missed it. No way had Rhapsody's mom climbed out of the window, but I'd pay money to see her try.

Too bad for me – she returned with a glass of ice water and handed the envelope to Courtney. "Take your money. I'm not leaving my daughter and her father."

She pressed the paper back into Ruby's hand. "You misunderstand," Courtney said with definite force. "You're in danger. This way you can choose where you go."

Ruby's eyes narrowed and she squeezed the envelope into a ball. "If we're in so much danger, then the *police* can protect us. Explain your bribe and identity to them!"

"She called the police." Courtney checked her fancy watch, as if she'd expected it. "Rhapsody, how far is the police station from here? Give me a tight ballpark."

"Umm. . .four or five minutes, nonstop through lights," she answered.

Courtney accessed the case she'd brought into the house by placing her thumbs on two black, square plates. The locks popped and she opened it. Inside was an impressive display of silver plated equipment. She tossed black packages wrapped in plastic, one to Rhapsody and another to me. "Two minutes. Put these on."

Rhapsody grabbed my hand and we ran into her bedroom. I felt nervous enough to throw up. I'd never undressed in a girl's room besides Sasha's, and even then we weren't doing much of anything.

She kicked off her leather boots and dropped her loose-fitting blue denim cut-offs and golf t-shirt to the floor. Beneath them she'd wore black spandex shorts and a purple bra with small holes on the sides. I tried not to look at her but she caught me.

"Don't wanna touch the merchandise, but window shopping is okay?" she asked while unwrapping the plastic. "Eventually you're gonna buy. That's how it works."

I didn't follow what she was saying, so I busied myself with dodging the junk spread out on her floor and unwrapping my package. It was some sort of flexible Kevlar body suit, like footie pajamas for adults. There were gloves and the shiny overlay looked like a metallic chain link skin. There was excess material at the top – a hoody? No, it was a mask.

I stepped into the suit, zipping it up just below my neck. Stashing my pouch of crystals in the inside breast pocket, I let the mask dangle at the back of my head. By the time I noticed it, Rhapsody was fully dressed. She was curvier than I thought.

When we left the bedroom our appearance spooked Ruby. Her eyes bulged and the skin on her arms and face shone with sweat, but she didn't try to stop us. Either our hidden lives were too interesting or she was in total shock.

Fortunately for us, we had experience with this type of thing.

"Jason." Courtney called my name from the back door, where she crossed her arms over her breasts and tapped her foot. I focused on her voice. Everything else faded. Rhapsody talked Spanish to Ruby nearby, but I did not hear them. "Jason?"

I blinked. The inside of my mouth dried and my skin tingled. "Yeah?"

"Focus," she said, touching my cheeks. Her palms were soft and smelled like citrus fruit. "North Hospital. Straight to room 313." She dropped the zipper on my suit and tucked a business card in the inside pocket behind the prisms. "Masks on – keep your speed up. Meet us at the coordinates on the card when you finish."

George's room used to be on the third floor, until they moved him to ICU on the fifth floor. I thought of the hospital's address. Just as soon as I did, it disappeared. I repeated it to myself twice to keep it fresh in my mind.

Courtney zipped me back up and pulled the mask over my head. It had mesh one-way viewing windows on the inside and a small rubber mouthpiece. "Good luck."

I ran out of the house, almost breaking the door off of the hinges as I did it. Rhapsody followed me. She whisked her hair into a bun and pulled her mask down. Both of us looked like two weirdoes in tight metal spandex, but Rhapsody's clung to every curve of her body. *Yep, I'm staring again.*

Courtney waved to the air and pointed. Holding Rhapsody much closer than I wanted to, we lifted off into the air. Police cars swerved to a stop in front of her house, where the neighbors had crowded together to watch whatever had just made a sonic boom.

Rhapsody placed a hand on my chest and made us invisible for our landing a few seconds after we ascended. Going supersonic made for quick travel.

Our feet never touched the roof of the hospital. We ghosted right through it, drifting through the top twelve floors and becoming solid on a level that looked familiar. It wasn't the third, which was our destination. I noticed an emerald green strip the width of my hand running along the edge of the freshly-mopped white floor. *Any shade of green, but especially that one, catches my eye now.*

I unmasked and the rubber mouthpiece hissed with leftover air. "We didn't go far enough, did we?" I whispered to her. "Which level are we on?"

"Five." She found my hand and pointed it ahead. "ICU is this way. Follow me."

"But Courtney said go to 313 first."

"She isn't here, is she?" Rhapsody said, annoyed. "Invisibility goes with me."

I remembered the plan. "Crystals go with *me*. 313 first."

Rhapsody cursed and shoved me in the shoulder before dropping us down two more levels without warning. My stomach dropped, and when we landed my insides shook. She could have warned me, but she was pissed and unreasonable.

Rounding the beige counter where the nurses stationed themselves, we followed the navy blue and white-lettered signs on the wall to the room.

She kept her hand at the small of my back, which I forced myself to accept as we walked down the white corridor. It reminded me that although our lives were in danger, things were still strange between us. We'd have to talk about the kiss some time.

When a pair of male doctors in green scrubs almost bumped into us, Rhapsody quickly turned us intangible. My heart seemed to stop every time someone walked *through* me. How had she gotten used to her new powers so fast? Were mine were more complicated, or was I somehow making it harder than it was?

Before peeking into Room 313, we examined the patient's medical chart like we knew what we were looking for. He was anonymous, nicknamed "John Doe." His admission date was May 8 – right after Reject High exploded. I didn't feel good about this. Still, I kept reading. His diagnosis was. . .*osteosarcoma?* "No," I said out loud.

Rhapsody nudged me. "That's the same kind of cancer Pápa has."

"Yeah. My mom had it, too."

Who was this guy?

Now visible and tangible, we proceeded forward. Rhapsody closed the heavy wooden door behind us.

A black-screened monitor beeped, followed by another one we couldn't pinpoint. A ventilator pumped air into his lungs. There was movement beneath his blue hospital gown. A few seconds later, it deflated. His body sagged. Another set of beeps seemed to echo in the room.

The door handle clicked, and Rhapsody turned us invisible again. A nurse peeked in, walked through us, looked around, walked back through us, and closed the door.

Both of us sighed. There wasn't much time. Never was.

I unzipped my suit and pulled it down far enough to retrieve the prisms. Once I got them out, Rhapsody dropped her powers. I'd use half of the emeralds on this guy. That's what Courtney needed us to do, I guessed. The other half were for George.

We moved closer to the bed and touched the silver guardrails. A large plastic bag of clear liquid dripped into an intravenous tube implanted in his right hand. His body was skeleton-thin and covered by wrinkled, dark brown skin. Even when the ventilator cycled on, he looked like that. He had these gross open sores dotting his forearms. Wild white hair covered his head, sprouted from his face and reached down to his chest.

"We don't have all day, Cap," Rhapsody said sharply over another set of beeps. "Get it over with. My dad's on a different floor."

"Don't rush me."

After pocketing the other crystals and zipping back up, I palmed fewer than half of the green emeralds and placed them underneath the mystery man's right hand. His skin was leathery, but dry, like it hadn't been moisturized in ages.

Nothing happened.

The ventilator did its work. Beeping and hissing continued.

Rhapsody grabbed my elbow. "Let's go. Now. . ."

She lingered on her last word when the stranger inhaled during an off-cycle for the ventilator.

He'd done it on his own.

After a few seconds it hit me that I'd stopped breathing and my heart had skipped a beat. Rhapsody didn't even have the presence of mind to curse, which she would have had done had she not been totally freaked out, like I was.

Suddenly his body arced, filling and stretching like a human balloon. Rhapsody turned her back to him. I had to watch.

It was way too intense to stop staring, but we backed away at the same time. The sores on his arms disappeared into completely healthy skin. He opened his eyes.

In that second I guessed who he was. *Peters*. Our old Physical Science teacher who had figured out we had powers and almost killed me three times. He was alive after all, but fighting Welker in the gym had left him like this. Courtney had tricked us into reviving a monster. Were they friends? Lovers?

"It's Peters," Rhapsody said. She held her arm out to push me back.

I should have let her push me, but after our last encounter with Peters, I could only think one thing.

Run.

Peters snatched the needle from his hand and pulled the ventilator tubing out of his mouth. "Wait," he said in a hoarse voice. "Don't!"

Rhapsody turned toward the door and ran through it. I followed her, except she had forgotten to turn me intangible. With a full running start, I smashed through the closed door, sending a heavy shower of dark brown splinters blasting into the hallway wall.

Everyone within a close distance ducked, except for a red-haired candy striper staring in my direction. Refusing to look at her, for fear she'd recognize my face, I pulled my mask down over my head.

"Sorry!" Rhapsody yelled from down the hall in a disguised voice. "You're fine!"

I swallowed hard and dashed full speed through the crowd, passing through the panicked bodies of doctors, orderlies, and nurses.

A brown-haired security guard with a phone in his hand called a "Code Black." He repeated it after we had run past him.

Code Black – that can't be good.

At the end of the hall I panted and whispered, "What . . . was *that?*"

"Lost control. . .for a second," Rhapsody managed to spit out. "502. C'mon."

Heat rushed to my collar. "Are you insane? How are we gonna get him out? You can't ghost all three of us."

Rhapsody was quiet for a moment. The ruckus surrounding us got louder. Every time we spoke people searched around for the source of the voices they could not find.

"I can't do it alone. I need you."

She sounded real, vulnerable. Not like she was giving me a line of crap, which she didn't do, anyway. And I knew she needed me, and better me than Selby this time.

"Okay." I held Rhapsody at the waist. With our powers working together, we made it to the fifth floor just in front of the elevators.

Side by side, we jogged over to George's room and passed through the closed door. His condition was similar to Peters', minus all of the hair. He didn't have any bedsores. The medicine drip was there, and so was the ventilator. Unlike where we came from, this floor was quieter and smelled of bleach cleaner and medicine.

Rhapsody appeared in front of me. Her red eyes brimmed with tears.

"Are you sure?" I flailed my hands. "This might not work."

She nodded and pursed her lips. "Do it. Please."

I lifted George's limp palm, cupped it so that he could hold them, and slowly emptied the bag of emeralds into his hand. Rhapsody took my place and held his fingers shut. Her eyes darted back and forth, from George to me and back to him.

Beep. Beep. His heart monitor was steady. The ventilator *pssshed*, whisking a steady stream of air into his lungs. His chest rose, then fell.

"Why isn't it working?" she asked. A renegade tear trailed down her cheek. "Peters woke up in a hurry," she cried. "Why's Pápa still laying there?"

I bit my lip to keep myself from saying what I really thought – George was brain dead. Our powers are wired to our minds. If his brain doesn't work, he might be gone.

We waited longer. The thin white drapes at the window moved in the cooling system's airflow, but I didn't need it. Every part of my body covered by the suit was the perfect temperature. Was it designed that way?

Moving my mouth to say something, I coughed instead. If Courtney and Peters had teamed up, she'd tell him where we were, and he'd come after us. Odds were that he'd have a hard time getting to us without exposing his powers.

I flexed and relaxed my fingers, focusing on the metallic crunching sound of the gray, scale-like plates on my gloves bumping against one another. In these suits we looked like futuristic comic book heroes.

George's condition did not change. More beeping and hissing.

I paced back and forth beside his bed to keep myself from screaming out at Rhapsody. Risking everything by standing here was kind of stupid, but if my mom had been lying there, I might've wanted someone to do the same thing for me.

Rhapsody's lips trembled. "Pápa," she muttered. She wiggled free of her suit enough to free her right arm. She stroked his face with her bare hand. "Please."

CHAPTER TEN

escape to the middle of nowhere

Ten minutes had passed, and nothing had happened. I'd kept my word.

The hospital staff might have thought my crash through Peters' door was faulty equipment. Even worse, a *bomb* or something. They would move the patients around.

Meaning we *really* had to go.

"Rhapsody." I spoke her name softly but with force. I had to get through to her.

She nodded, knowing what I intended to say. "A second."

I couldn't go out in the hallway dressed like I was going to Comic-Con, so I manned the door. I'd use my strength to hold it closed for now.

Rhapsody cursed and backed away from her father.

I flinched. Had he died? Trembling, she rambled in Spanish – a prayer? I couldn't really tell. My Spanish was terrible. The only reason I might have passed that class was an extra credit project I'd finished right before the school had blown up.

"What the h– ?"

Saying nothing, she pointed at George's hand – the one with the crystals. The color of its fingers flushed a healthy pinkish-brown color. Like Peters had done before him, George inhaled on his own. The crystals were working.

He blinked twice and turned his head toward Rhapsody, who dropped to the floor. George tugged at his ventilator tube with his left hand. "Ra. . .na," he mumbled.

Shock arrested my limbs. I froze, unable to do anything but stare. My thoughts rolled to a halt. I wished these crystals had existed back when my mother was this sick.

Rhapsody got to her feet without my help and rushed over to George, smothering him with kisses on the face. She stroked his sweaty head and smiled, her tears still falling. "You're gonna be okay, Pápa. You're getting out of here."

George rolled his head to the left and noticed me standing in the corner. I bowed my head. A month ago he'd asked me to take care of his daughter. Rhapsody and I had our ups and downs, but so far, I think I'd done okay – including being here now.

"H-how?" he asked. He must mean his ability to speak. Though I wondered why he hadn't reacted to the crystals the same way Peters did.

She pointed to his right hand. "That's how."

Two mint green-colored prisms hit the floor. When they lose power, their color fades from a dark shade to clear, like a diamond.

"These," she said, picking them up and holding one in front of his face. Jason, he'll get you as many as you need, and. . ."

George hacked and thrashed around on his bed. The heart monitors dinged double time as his pulse raced. Rhapsody steadied him as well as she could, but the prisms must have made him too strong for her to restrain.

"Don't just stand there!" she shrieked. "Help me. He's dropping them all."

I abandoned my post and rushed to his bedside. Holding George down without hurting him was difficult for me.

His eyes swelled with panicked tears. Not only did George know what the green emeralds did, but *they scared him. Why?*

"He's seen these before," I said. "Not when I gave him one. Before that."

"What?" Rhapsody picked up the crystals bouncing on the floor and placed them back into George's hand. "Have you seen these before?" she asked him.

His head wildly nodded. "Y-essss. . .bul. . .low. . . "

"Pápa," Rhapsody said, her voice trembling. "You're not making sense. 'Bul-low', what is that?"

She started with the Spanish again, but she spoke so slowly I understood bits and pieces of it. *Su carta* meant "your letter" – the one he wrote to her? Rhapsody had shown up at Aunt Dee's house a day after Reject High exploded. I gave it to her then. I hadn't read it, and we'd never talked about what George said in it.

Sniffling between sobs, Rhapsody talked a little faster, too fast for my amateur translation. Suddenly I remembered that I'd left the room unprotected. George had calmed down, so I left him in Rhapsody's hands and crossed the white linoleum floor.

Whatever she'd said to him, he'd lost the ability to respond. The color of his skin paled and darkened. I couldn't see the green emeralds from where I was standing, but by the look on Rhapsody's face, I knew they were quickly losing power.

The silver door handle clicked underneath my hand. I grabbed it before the person on the other side could enter. Whistling loudly enough to get Rhapsody's attention, I jerked my head toward the door. "Time's up," I mouthed to her.

"Not yet," she said, kissing George on the forehead. "You promised."

I'd given her my word to give him crystals every day, not to stand here and get caught by our enemies. He'd burned through most of what I'd harvested over the past month in less than twenty minutes. At that rate, no way I could keep him alive until the crystals exploded, even though I wanted to do it. We needed to revise the game plan.

Rhapsody touched her father's chest and leaned her head against his.

Suddenly she perked up. Had George said something? She pulled the ventilator tube fully away from his lips. I didn't hear anything and couldn't see his mouth, but the back of his neck tensed, then relaxed.

As I watched them my right leg buckled. Compensating with my left, I found it difficult to breathe, like I'd been stabbed in the side. My powers were slipping away. Someone outside of the room was using goshenite against me.

"Have to. . ." I tried to yell. My normal strength wasn't enough. With another push from the other side, I'd smash into the wall. Whoever it was would have us in custody.

Rhapsody laid her midsection across George's chest and sobbed.

That's it. We're done. Our enemies have won.

I closed my eyes and waited for the final push.

When I dared to look again, Rhapsody was dropping us down through the hospital floors. We stopped falling when my shoes smacked hard against the concrete parking deck. Waving my hands to the sides, I steadied myself, and then I patted my chest.

I was invisible.

The choking scent of car exhaust and gasoline was strong. I looked around – we were on the deck's bottom level.

My friend was nowhere to be seen. Where was she?

"Rhapsody?" I called out. All I heard was the shallow echo of my own voice. I yelled her name again, patting the cold, gray concrete. "Are you here? Are you hurt?"

Silence.

"Answer me!" I screamed long and hard, at the top of my lungs.

"I'm here," she said in a shaky, small voice.

I tried to guess where her voice came from. "Well, I can't see you."

Although it was the middle of the afternoon, the closed-in level was dark, except for lights at the corners where people would make turns. The tubes in the ceiling in front of me had blown out, and Rhapsody's voice originated somewhere behind me.

I reached my hands out for her and stated the obvious again. "We gotta go. We're sitting ducks down here."

Rhapsody's emotions were all over the place. She couldn't control her powers enough to reappear.

I followed the audible trail of her tears. Finding her calf first, I patted the ground until I reached her other leg. Gently, I picked her up in my arms. Still invisible, she nuzzled close to me. The smell of her flowery perfume was strong. Holding her made me feel odd, but I put that aside. My best friend needed me.

I carried her to the edge of the parking lot and kicked the wall, sending chunks of concrete and metal wiring flying with each kick. Once I'd made a big enough hole, we stepped through it onto the sidewalk. Above us, the bright yellow sun shone. In broad daylight anyone could see us, recognize us. I hoped we looked good online for whoever was going to film us.

Looking down at my feet, I saw Rhapsody had pulled it together and turned me invisible. It was a good thing. Policemen had set up red and white roadblock barriers in both directions. They crowded the streets, wearing black riot gear. Several black police vans lined the street. I wondered if they were packing white ice.

"Unzip my suit," I said, rushing her into an alleyway. "Reach into the inside pocket for a card."

Rhapsody sniffed. My suit loosened and separated as she tugged at the zipper. Soon she had slipped her hand against my sweaty t-shirt and finished the job. She placed the card into my right palm.

I let her stand on her own and backed away, hoping the distance would turn me visible. Sure enough, it worked.

Besides the word "Walsh," I read a series of numbers and dashes – coordinates. Other than the "E," which meant east, I had no idea where to go. *How am I supposed to read these? Perfect.* I hid the truth of my confusion from Rhapsody. She didn't need to know.

Two hours away in the middle of nowhere was the perfect place for a secret hideout. Walsh was a farming town with nothing around but corn fields and Hidden Potential a.k.a. "the Black Hole" – a boot camp for problems waiting to happen, like me. Vivienne Coker ran it. People said it was *worse* than going to Reject High. Once a kid goes in the Black Hole, he doesn't come out until he turns eighteen, and she has to free him.

After mumbling the coordinates to myself a few times I found Rhapsody sitting on the ground with her back against the grime-caked brick alley wall. Her chest and shoulders spasmed every couple seconds. She stopped weeping. I was surprised she had any tears left after crying so much. "My mom had to go and flush my last cigarette. Figures."

I held out my gloved hand to her. "I can't do this alone," I said. "I need you, too."

Rhapsody's face brightened a little. She grabbed my hand and I helped her up. "Funny." Her voice evened out. "Somebody smart must've told you that."

I pocketed the card. "We're supposed to go to Walsh. Wanna blow it off because of that whole Peters thing?"

Her face screwed with displeasure. "Right. Can't be someplace we might *want* to go either. Why can't we get sent to someplace fancy, like Xobai or something?"

Maybe Courtney had a good reason. "Do you trust her?"

Rhapsody hissed. "She told you to wake up the dude who tried to kill you."

She had a point. "You alright?"

"Not really."

Walsh was west of town and we were facing east. I brought us to the flat roof of the hospital, where the trauma center had a landing pad for its helicopter. Thankfully no one was around in the tower. Rhapsody turned us invisible, anyway.

I looked over the edge. There were *dozens* of police officers roaming the street with assault rifles. Were they all looking for me and Rhapsody?

We were stuck – we couldn't go back home, either.

Rhapsody squatted next to me. "I'll never see him alive again," she said.

There was nothing for me to say. I rubbed my gloved hand back and forth across where I thought her shoulders would be. She got to see him, which was a good thing.

She continued, stopping every few words. "Pápa hated me Goth – got me bullied by Asia and her bobble-head groupies. No disrespect."

Sasha hung out with Asia, who had died in that explosion to save us.

"He cut off the Internet on my phone. I didn't see it online," she muttered. "Kids thought me and Cherish were lesbians. She was. I'm not. I like guys."

I hadn't heard those rumors, though Ruby had mentioned it once a while ago.

Rhapsody's voice cracked. "Nobody's ever done something like that for me and my dad before – until today. Thanks."

"No worries," I said.

She stood and hugged me, wrapping her arms behind my back. I squeezed her tight enough to say, "You don't disgust me," but not enough for, "you're smoking hot in this tight body suit."

Both of us heard the sound of a helicopter approaching.

"Ready?" I asked, pulling my mask down. "I need some answers for all of this."

Rhapsody did the same. "Yeah."

Holding her tight, I took us from the roof, heading west toward Walsh.

CHAPTER ELEVEN

conspiracy theories 101

Walsh was at least forty-five minutes away from the hospital, but we arrived there much in less time. Because of our masks, Rhapsody and I could breathe at high speeds.

Somewhere along the line, I lost my concentration – maybe my Adderall was wearing off early. So when we descended into a field of corn and knee-high weeds we were going too fast and came down hot. The landing was rough and *really* loud. My feet kicked up clods of brown dirt.

Rhapsody slid down out of my arms, unmasked, and shook out the cobwebs from her head. "Okay then."

"Don't know what happened." I yanked off my mask and walked off my annoyance.

She unzipped her suit down to her stomach, leaned over and panted.

I forced myself not to look.

"You're. . .fine," she said out of breath.

Around us the weeds and cornstalks waved in the breeze. The sun overhead beat down on us, but the temperature seemed bearable. We stared at each other.

"It must have a cooling system," I muttered. "We went supersonic and they didn't shred." I wondered what else they were capable of doing. Looking around, I spotted nothing but field as far as I could see.

Rhapsody, who still looked shaken, raised her eyebrows. "This is right?" she asked me. "What the card said?"

I shrugged. *How do I think of an address, even in places I'd never been, and always end up there? The crystals?* Courtney had given me coordinates, not a street or house number. Maybe that had screwed up my mental GPS. "I didn't read it wrong, if that's what you mean," I lied. "It's not like there's a mailbox around."

"All right," Rhapsody said.

She and I searched in opposite directions for *anything* – a trap door, blinking lights. Courtney could have given us a hint. The card didn't say anything beyond numbers and a general direction. I couldn't tell if we were even in the right spot.

Frustrated, I stomped my right foot once, making the ground shake.

In the distance, Rhapsody steadied herself. By the time the tremor stopped, I wondered if I had started an actual earthquake. We hadn't had one in a year.

My friend was about a quarter mile away. "I found something," she said.

Taking a measured leap, I touched down next to her. She pointed at the ground. The weeds were smashed down in two parallel lines a couple of feet apart. Tire tracks. The marks disappeared in front of us.

Whatever it was, it was underneath the surface.

I knelt down and forced my hand down into the dirt, stopping at a hard metal surface half a foot down. Right when I was about to dig my fingers in and pull it, we heard gears whirring and churning, like a giant machine's moving parts.

Rhapsody and I backed up.

Looks like I can read coordinates after all.

A platform the width of a two-lane road slowly rose from the ground. Clumps of dirt and grass dropped down from the edge of the opening. A loud *snap* and series of rapid clicks told us the gateway had finished lifting itself. Now high enough for us to walk in without having to duck or crawl, the corridor lit up from its sides. *A tunnel?* We had to get closer to be sure.

Rhapsody looked at me to make the call.

I took the lead.

The hallway smelled of oil, engine exhaust, and moldy earth. Its sputtering orange lights were bright enough to light our path. Rhapsody and I moved slowly.

She reached for my hand more than once. "Take my hand, dude," she said with force.

I did it. She squeezed tightly. I was afraid, too. My heart pounded in my throat.

We reached a freight elevator and stepped inside. I pushed the "B" button, thinking it would take us to the basement, if it didn't explode or drop us thirty floors to our death.

The elevator clanked and rattled into position. The passageway closed in front of us – much more quickly than it had opened. It made me think of an old movie I'd seen once, where two robots went into a dark building in the middle of nowhere. Of course, they didn't die, because they couldn't.

"Where *are* we?" Rhapsody asked.

Two of the levels we passed were submerged in total blackness. The only things visible to us were gigantic, sharp shadows the size of small buildings. From their angles, I thought they might be airplanes or jets. The scent of fuel and oil reinforced that idea, so maybe it wasn't an off-the-mark crazy hunch, after all. Based on my last one, I'd bet Ray that San Francisco would beat Los Angeles in a baseball game, and when they lost by fifteen runs, I was stuck hand-washing his Cougar.

I'm glad I didn't say, "Are those planes?" out loud. Rhapsody was a grieving mess, but she'd have jumped all over that one.

A US Air Force logo gleamed on the elevator's rusted control panel, catching my eye. Underneath it was a faded metal plate with "BAE.A.T." in red block letters. *Wonder what it stands for?*

Unlike regular elevators, this one loudly smacked against the metal housing bolted to the floor.

"*Ding,*" I joked. "Secret lair. Bottom floor."

We proceeded into a deserted room with thick metal beams and bolts connected to the ceiling. Rusted orange rectangular marks lined its walls. The gray dust was so thick it looked as if someone had clapped a million chalkboard erasers in here. My nose tingled from it, like I'd sneeze at any second.

Still holding my hand, Rhapsody squeezed it. Ahead of us was a narrow door. *Where does it go?* Since we'd come this far, I didn't see any point in turning around.

Wherever it went, we had to continue forward to find out. Turning the knob with my left hand, I made sure not to pull too hard. It opened to a walkway so narrow that Rhapsody couldn't walk next to me. She trailed behind, her fingers locked in mine. The scent of gasoline was gone, replaced by something just as strong – a chemical that smelled like the world's largest cough drop. Almost choking on the stuffy air, I sniffed it. "What *is* that?"

"Cleaner, maybe?" Rhapsody asked from behind me, her voice shaking.

I turned to look at her. Her eyes shifted back and forth. She was thinking something else that the smell was from a substance way more dangerous than cleaner.

The walkway continued through to another passageway and another, like subway cars. None of them were well-lit. We paced through them all. Any kind of loud noise might have sent me through the roof. But I wouldn't leave Rhapsody alone to face whatever.

The last pathway let us into what appeared to be the living area of an underground compound. Through that was a kitchen with silver walls and futuristic-looking appliances. I think there was a refrigerator, or a large shiny cabinet of some kind. Was there an apple pie cooking somewhere? The scent of apples and cinnamon made my stomach growl.

"*Food,*" Rhapsody grunted the word like she hadn't eaten in weeks. "I recognize *that* smell. Pit stop?"

"We'll be back." I mentally marked the place – if there was anything edible in there, even if it was just a small pie, we'd eat it.

Stumbling into the garage, we found the black late model van with tinted windows I'd seen parked outside of Aunt Dee's next to an old motorcycle and a black vintage Cougar sedan.

Through the next passageway we found what we were looking for.

I stepped in first, while Rhapsody followed close me. The area was completely circular with a ten-foot-high ceiling. Spaced in a half circle bordering the round walls were tall bookcases. In front of them were desks made of red wood, with large computer monitors. The other side looked like a hospital room with curtains, beds, and monitors. That's where we sensed movement.

Courtney was the first to notice us. She had been kneeling, I guess to fine-tune some equipment. She stood when she heard us. "Welcome," she said with a smirk. She wore the same business suit we'd seen her in a while ago. "Thanks for knocking first."

Sasha sat on an examining table next to Courtney. She looked different with no makeup and her hair frizzed and combed back. She wore a black snakeskin adult footie pajama suit like ours. Her weary smile drooped when she saw Rhapsody and me connected at the hand. We pulled apart, but I was sure she and I would have a discussion about it later.

At least she didn't know about the kiss. Wait, did she sense it? Could she?

I pretended everything was okay and rushed over, but she signaled that I shouldn't touch her. "Don't," she said stiffly. "I cleaned up Corky's puke for hours. And you were with *her* all this whole time?"

Rhapsody crossed her arms across her chest when Sasha gestured in her direction.

I defended her. "She tricked us into waking up Peters and George just. . ."

"*Then,*" she interrupted me, still venting. "Janitor Brad breaks into my house and grabs me like a *Lifetime* movie. I can't! You two, Joyce, this, it's just too. . ."

The mention of our old janitor made me tilt my head. "Wait, *what?* 'Janitor Brad'?"

Across the room and with his back to us, the guy kind of *did* look like Janitor Brad. He was tall, kind of thin, dark-skinned and bald. His white dress shirt was unbuttoned below his neck and his black tie hung loosely beneath it.

"Name's Hughes," he said loudly enough for all of us to hear. "Not Brad."

When Hughes turned around I noticed that his black and gray goatee was shaped like Brad's. He wore eyeglasses. Brad didn't. Without them he could have been Brad's identical twin. The janitor never talked to me, so I didn't know his voice.

Whoever this guy was, I needed answers. "Are we even safe here, wherever *here* is?" I asked. "I saw the Air Force symbol. I thought you weren't government?"

Hughes sighed. "Safe? For the most part. And we're not government."

Rhapsody bristled at the answer. "Little more vague?"

"What he means," Courtney said. "Is that safety's only an issue when you're not more powerful than whoever is after you. As long as we're around, the answer is yes.

"This is an old government facility we commandeered. President Clinton shut it down before he left office. It's been ours ever since."

"The least he could've done for us," said Hughes. I wondered what he meant.

"Who's after us? Who is it?" Sasha's body shook. *"Tell me!"*

Whoever it is, it better not be Peters. Which reminded me, "Your buddy from the hospital? Him?" I asked Courtney. "Peters?"

"Think, Jason. He's not your enemy," Hughes said. He almost sounded sincere.

I laughed. "Your friends try to kill you?"

"He's much more of a help than a danger," Courtney said with a straight face.

"That's debatable," shouted the Asian woman from behind one of the curtains. Her shadow jerked and shifted, like the mention of Peters' name made her jumpy.

"He's one of us," Courtney shot back. "Camuto's joking."

"No," Camuto said. She rounded the curtain and stared at me over her glasses. She, too, was dressed the same way Courtney and Hughes were. "Camuto is *not joking.*"

Three months ago he'd shot at us, nearly hit me with a car, and tried to choke me to death. I believed her.

Sasha scooted to the end of the table. I tried to help her down. "I got it," she said, shooing me with her hands. "It's two feet to the floor. I'll be fine."

I snapped. "What's your problem? You told me to leave and I left."

"I didn't know *where* you were going or with whom!" she shrieked. "Seriously, her over me?"

Sasha obviously meant with Rhapsody. "You should shut up. *Now,*" I told her.

She slapped me across the cheek too quickly for me to drop my powers. Sasha cursed and shook her hand in pain.

"I helped Rhapsody say goodbye to George," I said over her grumbling.

Still massaging her right hand, Sasha gazed over at Rhapsody. She must have finally noticed the pain in Rhapsody's eyes that had been there for the past hour.

"Alright," she said, still wincing. "I'll shut up now."

The awkward silence among the three of us stretched on for hours. Okay, it might have actually been a minute or less, but no one said a word, not even our hosts. Hughes monkeyed around with a piece of equipment. Camuto disappeared behind the curtain. From her demeanor, I could tell why Rhapsody started calling Camuto "Sour Lemon Face" behind her back. The woman couldn't smile. And Courtney, for some odd reason, watched us interact like we were experiments in a Petri dish. Hadn't she seen teenagers before?

CHAPTER TWELVE

pink is the color of danger

Still silent, Hughes left us alone with Courtney in the giant circular room. She flashed us a weird, toothy grin. Were we a joke to her?

"Hungry?" she asked.

The aroma of the apple pie and cinnamon flashed in my memory, making my stomach clench in anticipation.

Rhapsody's must have, too. She licked her lips. "Totally," she said.

"I could eat," Sasha chimed in.

"Hughes likes to cook more than the rest of us do. He's very thorough, though, so it'll be a while before we actually sit down and get a chance to talk. You can hang out here."

She disappeared behind the beds, wires, and medical equipment. I spotted a double-sided, ten-foot-high cabinet back there that I hadn't noticed before. "Incoming!" she yelled.

Courtney tossed food to us – bags of chips and cheese crackers, toaster pastries, breakfast bars, trail mix, and gummy fruit snacks.

"How did you know?" I asked her, sounding dramatic on purpose.

"Eat up," she said. "Don't be shy."

Rhapsody barely hesitated before opening the bags in her hands. Neither did I. Even after using her powers Sasha picked at her food in a steady, nonstop stream instead of gobbling it down, like we did.

"Give me that." Rhapsody snatched a bag of fried onions from my arms. She replaced it with honey roasted pretzels.

"Hey, Rhapsody, I'm sorry," Sasha said. Her apology sounded sincere. "If there's anything I can do, just. . ."

"I'm good, Sasha."

Did she just call Sasha by her name and not some sarcastic nickname? I don't think Rhapsody was blowing her off, but it was clear she didn't want to talk about it.

Sasha scrunched her brow and pointed to the two of us. "What was that, Goth Girl? Why did you just take those onion things from him?"

"Mmm," Rhapsody mumbled while chewing a candy bar. "He hates them. I thought it was a breath thing, but you'd know about his dragon mouth better than anyone else would."

I think I should have been offended, but Rhapsody's joke was a sign she was feeling better. "And don't call me *Goth Girl*," she added. "Lamey Lame here can't come up with something better to call me."

"Lamey Lame?" I opened my mouth and breathed in Rhapsody's face. "Rawr!"

She giggled and held her nose. "Your breath smells like rotten meatloaf!"

I laughed. Rhapsody doubled over chuckling.

But it looked like Sasha wasn't amused.

"Let me check." Sasha put her hand on the back of my neck and pulled me in for a kiss. Afterward she pretended to blow a smoke ring.

"Neither one of you cared before!" I blurted without thinking.

Almost immediately I started coughing. Rather than pat me on the back because I'm invulnerable, Sasha and Rhapsody watched me choke. My eyes welled with tears. I pounded my chest with my fist. I finally spit out the tiny pretzel fragment causing the trouble. By the time I did Sasha was nowhere to be seen.

Rhapsody handed me a cold plastic bottle of water. "Awkward."

I uncapped the bottle and swallowed half of its contents. Sasha knows. I didn't have an idea what to do when it happened, but I couldn't avoid discussing anymore. "I'm going after her," I said.

"Okay," Rhapsody said softly. "We'll talk about it later?"

It being the kiss. I held out my pinkie finger. "If you swear you won't follow me."

She hesitated for a second before locking pinkies with me. "Alright."

Thinking Sasha wasn't going to head back to the surface, I tried the other door leading out of the big round room. At the end of another narrow walkway, I found myself in a small, square room with two doors facing each other.

I chose the one to my left, which eventually dead-ended into the living quarters. There was a large screen

TV mounted into the far wall and plush burgundy couches facing it. Wonder if they have cable down here?

Backtracking to the square room, I took the other door. Two passageways later, I found a locked door. I gazed through its window and saw Sasha staring at the morganite, the pink provenance crystal. From a distance its prisms glowed with the color of a full-bloom carnation.

I pounded my fist against the metal door. Sasha didn't move. *How did she get inside?* I put my hand through the window and unlocked it from the inside. "Sasha?"

When the heavy metal door slammed behind me I thought she'd at least look my way or acknowledge my presence.

Instead, she didn't move.

"Are you okay?" When I neared the pink source I noticed the morganite were a shocking pink with gleaming edges. Next to it was a row of five holes in the wall. Had all of the source crystals been here at one point?

"It's beautiful, isn't it?" she asked me.

"Yeah, whatever," I said, ignoring it. "Can we talk about this?"

"Talk about what, Jason?"

Was this a game or did she want me to confess? "I kissed Rhapsody." Sweat broke out on my forehead. "Well, she actually kissed me. I didn't stop her." My voice lowered. "Look, we kissed and I'm sorry."

Sasha turned to look at me, tears rolling down her cheeks. The rose pink light reflected off of her body. It was almost hypnotic. A stream of thoughts came pouring out my brain, thoughts of kissing Sasha, of doing more than kissing her, of beating up Selby and throwing Ray's Cougar into the Pacific. They were difficult to control.

While her eyes stayed on me, her expression was completely blank. Her emotions were completely unreadable.

"Do you like her?" she asked, dragging out the words of her question.

The right answer was no. The wrong answer was yes. I hesitated for a second. In this case, it was worse than lying or telling the truth. "No, not at all." I'd pray to God for forgiveness and deal with the nagging in my gut later.

Still crying, Sasha regained her focus and looked me in the eye. "Did it mean something to you?"

This time I answered correctly for her. "No."

Sasha surrounded me in a hug. "She's dealing with a lot and you were there for her," she said, like she was trying to convince herself it was the truth.

"Yeah."

Sasha stepped away from me. "But you can't be alone with her again."

Under normal circumstances that seemed like a reasonable request. Days out from a nuclear explosion, however, were not normal circumstances. Sweat formed at my neck above my suit's collar. "How am I supposed to do that here, Sasha? Down here, eventually it'll happen."

She bit her lip. "If Selby came down here, would you want me alone with him?"

I flashed back to the couple seconds of their sex tape I saw. "It's different," I said with force. "You and he, you. . ."

"It's *the same,*" she countered.

"Me and Rhapsody kissed. We didn't have sex on the Internet!" I yelled.

It was a low blow, but I couldn't take it back now. She cursed at me and fanned out her hands. "Whatever. Do what you want to do. Oh yeah, you already did that."

I circled behind her. "I apologized and said what you wanted me to say. What else do you want from me?"

Sasha bit her lip. "The truth, not what you think I want to hear!"

While we argued, Camuto stepped around the broken glass and ran over to us. "Get away from *that*," she said, waving her arms. She stayed at a distance.

"What? Why?" I slid back a foot or so. Sasha backed against the far wall.

"Why are you down here?" she asked, her nostrils flaring.

"Because we needed to talk," Sasha wiped her face and raised an eyebrow. "Privately."

"There are thirty-plus corridors in this compound, seven people, and you pick this one?" Camuto pointed to the source. "Did you harvest any of these?"

It's not the first time I'd been accused of stealing. "What's your problem? Look, lady, we didn't take any prisms."

"Prove it. Empty your pockets."

I unzipped my suit and showed her what was in my shorts' pockets – money, keys, and an old bus pass I used to support my lies to Aunt Dee. Sasha produced a tampon and her house keys. When I eyed the tampon she gave me a death stare, like she knew *exactly* what I was thinking.

"Alright," Camuto said. "In the future have your little teenager docudramas elsewhere. You don't do it in here, got it?"

I had to know. "Is this crystal more powerful than the green? What can you do with it?"

Camuto put her hands on her hips. "Nothing."

"The green gives us our abilities," Sasha said. "Using white can take them away, and the red is mind control and telekinesis. C'mon, the pink has to do *something.*"

Camuto's face hardened with anger. "Stay away from it."

Her reluctance to answer sent my curiosity through the roof. "How about this – you tell us, or I'll just take some and find out myself?"

She didn't respond. Was she calling my bluff? Something stirred inside me, like a warning to back off. Usually I ignored it and acted anyway. This time I didn't.

Camuto walked through the glass and held the door open from the outside. Obviously she didn't trust us to leave on our own. "Let's go."

"So, what now?" I asked Sasha as we walked out.

"I don't know, Jason."

We could break up or stay together. At this point I'm glad the kiss was out in the open, so I didn't have to hide it anymore. On the other hand, it gave Sasha another reason to hate Rhapsody more than she already did. What was it between them, anyway?

Sasha and I calmly talked about it as Camuto led us back to the giant circle. Courtney was gone. Rhapsody sat on one of the beds, her feet dangling over the edges. She'd taken off her suit and was in her spandex shorts and a long white t-shirt. Her upper body gently shook every few seconds. She was crying.

Sasha extended her right hand to me as a peace offering. I grabbed it. Together, we approached Rhapsody, who quickly tried to clear the tears from her face with some tissue.

"It's okay. We're here," Sasha said to her. "Go ahead and get it out."

We dropped hands and she draped her arm over Rhapsody's shoulders.

I patted my friend's left leg and she placed her warm hand over mine. For a quick second Rhapsody looked at me with hurt in her reddened eyes. Enough for me to know George's condition wasn't the only thing tearing her up inside.

CHAPTER THIRTEEN

Rhapsody vs. Sasha, round one

Rhapsody pulled away from us and blotted her face dry with tissues. "Bathroom?"

"There." I pointed behind her. "Keep going until you get to the bunks. There's probably a bathroom in there."

"Thanks, Cap." Rhapsody's lips curled into a tight smile. She slid off of the bed. "Be right back."

We were alone, except for Sour Lemon Face, a.k.a. Camuto, who pretended to be busy at her desk. Sasha and I still hadn't really reached an understanding about our relationship. Were we dating? On a break? I didn't want to know.

After unzipping and stepping out of my suit, I asked Camuto about a cell or Internet signal.

She stopped reading. "Three stories underground?" Camuto asked. "I'm going to go out on a limb and say no. We do have universal chargers, though."

Without an operational phone to distract me, there was really no reason not to talk to Sasha, unless she didn't want to talk either. No such luck.

"Truth, Jason?" She shook her head at me. "Rhapsody's liked you since your first day at Reject High. She made out with you in the cafeteria, in front of everybody, for God's sake. And she just kissed you again. Do you need her to hold up a sign?"

I remembered. "The first one was because Selby was coming to *cut me.*"

"Why didn't she tell you, 'heads up', 'watch out', or 'run away', even?"

She had a point – Selby was almost as slow as I am. "I don't know, Sasha."

"Yes, you do. Think about all the times she invited you over to her house. Why would she do that when you told me she was ashamed of it? You think Welker's safe is the only thing she wanted you to open?"

"Hold up." Rhapsody was still my friend. "It's not like that."

"Maybe it always was 'like that' and you ignored it – I did." She paused. "Tell me you *didn't* see she liked you, Jason, and I'll believe it. But now that you know, if nothing changes between the two of you, I'll know where we stand."

Before I could tell her what I really thought, Hughes shouted, "Soup's on!" over the antique loudspeaker system in the compound. Rhapsody appeared with her black hair loose and down past her shoulders. I glanced at both girls and made up my mind to sit as far away as possible during dinner.

The three of us filed into the kitchen. Awaiting us was a buffet table with any kind of delicious food we could want – six full-size pizzas: two with pepperoni, two with sausage, and two just cheese. Next to them were three containers of fried chicken wings. Hughes had also roasted a side of beef and carved it. There were vegetables: collard greens, sweet potatoes, mashed potatoes, baby corn, seared asparagus, garden and Caesar salad. There were biscuits, rolls, and a dessert table I couldn't even begin to comprehend.

Camuto grabbed a plate first. Rhapsody and Sasha followed. They kept their distance from each other by moving on opposite sides of the table. Hughes and I brought up the rear. I piled food on my plate carefully so nothing would drop.

Unfortunately, the dining room table seated eight and it wasn't situated for my plan. While the girls got drinks from the refrigerator, I sneaked over to the table to stake my claim.

"That's *my* seat," Hughes said, poking his head in from the kitchen. He wasn't wearing his glasses. I seriously suspect he was either Janitor Brad or Janitor Brad's rude twin. "Camuto sits to my left and Stafford's to my right. She's bringing someone, so skip a chair."

I was confused. "Dude, why does it even matter where we sit? It's not kindergarten," I said to him.

"Because it does," he growled.

Sitting next to Camuto meant there was a fifty percent chance I could avoid sitting next to Rhapsody or Sasha, so I took it. Sasha came in next and paused, counting the seats across from me with her eyes. She chose to sit next to Courtney's guest.

Rather than be arm's length from Sasha, Rhapsody settled in next to me. All things considered, this little arrangement could've turned out worse. I got up from the table and opened the refrigerator for a drink. While I had my head buried in the shelves, searching for a Sprite, Courtney and her guest arrived.

"Just in time," she said. "Get yourself a plate, Michael."

Michael? I cursed and accidentally hit my head against the handle of the freezer door, denting it. With two Sprite cans in hand, I returned to the dining room.

Selby was loading his plate with pizza when we crossed paths. "Oh, hey, Freak."

It was the first time I'd seen him since he'd almost killed me. If he wasn't faster than light, I'd have tossed both of my cans at his head. *"Leslie,"* I said, hoping his first name got under his skin as much as "Freak" did to me. "Where have you been?"

He let it pass. She must have tased him or something. "A better question is where *haven't* I been? And why did I come here to get stuck with you and them?"

"We need all of you," Courtney said to me in private. "Let's eat."

I returned to my seat and focused on satisfying my roaring appetite. Nobody said anything for a long time. We were too busy chewing and drinking.

I'd cleared a third of my plate when Rhapsody poked me in the leg and said "Courtney" under her breath.

"Huh?" I looked up. Selby and Sasha were sharing a laugh and looking in my direction. Whatever he said was stupid because he was stupid, but she laughed. Did he think I wouldn't turn this table over, rip it in half and beat him like a Whack-A-Mole?

"Jason, you asked how I knew you'd be this hungry. Remember?"

"Oh, yeah," I finished chewing the pizza crust in my mouth. What was so funny?

"The crystals you wear key off of the epinephrine, or adrenaline in your body," Courtney explained. "Your powers speed up most of your biological processes."

That explained why I burned through my Adderall so fast sometimes. "Oh."

"Why do they work on us and nobody else on the planet?" For once, Selby had asked an intelligent question. We all wanted to know the answer to it. "Is it all beryl?"

Camuto answered him. "We estimate there are about seven hundred of us. And no, not *all beryl*. Only prisms harvested from the provenance crystals."

"We have a rare protein in our blood which we can't isolate or synthesize," Courtney added. "It metabolizes the prism's radiation and lets us to do what we do."

"How do you know all this?" I turned and asked her.

"Because we've done the research," Camuto snapped. "We're not new to this."

Why is her attitude crappy all of the time? "Yeah? How long have you 'done research'?"

Camuto dropped her plastic fork. "A hundred years!" she shouted.

Sasha grinned. "The research is that old? They haven't personally tried to crack the code that long. I mean, that's not possible."

Her lack of a response stunned us into silence for the rest of the meal. Sasha, Selby, Rhapsody, and I looked at each other. Were they on drugs? *One hundred years? Seriously? That's impossible.* Though a lot of weird things had happened to us in the past month, eating dinner with three people that old topped the list.

Camuto left the table first, followed by Hughes. He worked on washing the pots in the kitchen. Courtney piled our used plates, cans, and utensils and then disappeared. We mouthed words to each other but did not dare to speak out loud.

Selby slapped the table and whispered, "Should've jetted when I had the chance. Now I'm stuck down here with *you* and three Crypt Keepers."

"Don't blame me," Rhapsody said. "We got invited to this party just like you did. They're not a hundred years old. That's not even possible."

"Yeah. Even so, if they've been researching that long, they'd have to be at least 120 years old, I'd think," Sasha said.

Her constant correction ticked Rhapsody off. "Really, Girl Genius? Do you have to correct me, like right now?"

Sasha rolled her neck. "Right now, Baby Girl. I've got it right here for you."

Rhapsody chuckled. "Not bad for a chick from the 'burbs with a picket fence."

"Heifer, I will drag your big hips up and down this place!"

The two of them pushed off from the table and stood up, facing each other.

I motioned for Sasha not to come to our side of the table. "Seriously. *Stop.*"

"I didn't start it." She balled her fists. "I'm gonna finish it, though."

"Let 'em fight," Selby said. "Chick fights are awesome, especially if they strip."

Sasha sent Clone Sasha behind us. She smacked Rhapsody hard on the back of the head. Rhapsody stumbled forward a little and cursed. On the next swing Rhapsody went intangible and Clone Sasha missed completely. She lost her balance and fell backwards onto the floor, knocking her head against the table's edge.

Rhapsody ghosted across the room and stood toe to toe with Original Sasha, who cloned herself seven more times. Then Rhapsody grabbed her at the shoulders and head-butted her. Sasha lost her concentration and all of the clones disappeared.

"Stop it," Courtney said.

Thankfully she used white ice on the girls and not us. I had too many injuries to deal with, and last I remembered, I'd broken some of Selby's ribs, so he probably didn't need the added pain, either.

"Follow me."

We trailed Courtney back to the pink source corridor. "Keep your distance," she said once we got inside. "Five feet or more. Any less and you'll absorb the radiation."

"What's so bad about that?" Selby asked. "Are you really a hundred years old?"

Rhapsody shushed him. "She might tell us, if you let her talk, Fool."

"Camuto didn't tell you what this one does because she didn't think you could handle it. I have more faith in you than she does. Pink beryl releases your innermost desire at the moment and makes you act on it."

Still rubbing her forehead, Sasha asked, "Why is that so dangerous?"

"Because most people don't know what that is about themselves," Courtney said. "Think of how dangerous you would be with powers and no inhibitions, the sorts of problems you would create."

Selby smiled.

Out of the corner of my eye, I saw a flash of recognition in Rhapsody's face. Had she seen this thing somewhere? "So what are you having faith in us to do?" I asked.

"Tomorrow, you – the four of you – will work together with us to collect the provenance crystals. We have a containment dome where they can safely detonate."

There was only one small problem with her plan. "What about King?"

"He's after them, too," she said. "We have to get to them first."

CHAPTER FOURTEEN

I finally get to sleep

Selby cracked his knuckles, like he was readying for a fight. "Who's this King, anyway?"

Courtney continued speaking in the faint glow of the pink source. "We all had. . . families." Her voice broke. "He's one of us. Six – we're all that's left."

"How?" Rhapsody asked. *"Why?"*

"The level of that protein in your blood – it drops tremendously after you turn eighteen. It's gone completely by the time you turn twenty-one."

My insides froze. I was almost afraid to ask. "Meaning?"

She licked her lips. "You'll have to make a choice, like we did."

Rhapsody glanced at the pink source. Her nostrils flared. "What kind of choice? Sophie's choice?"

"If you want to stay this way, of course." Courtney rubbed the back of her neck. "Imagine living life like gods on earth, doing all the things you can do with powers."

"Heck yeah!" Selby said, pumping his fist.

"Or spending your days with your loved ones, normal, dreaming about what you could have done being. . .exceptional."

From the looks on everyone's faces, we didn't want to pick either, especially Selby, who was two years older than us. "Well, what happens to us if we keep our crystals past eighteen and then take them off?" he asked.

"Under normal circumstances, the radiation causes incurable forms of cancer," she said, her voice losing its power. "That's what happens if the rest of the population wears them, Michael. For you, if you take them off then, you'll die."

The word *cancer* hit home for me and Rhapsody, silencing us both. I put my hands into my shorts' pockets. This was a lot to take in all at once.

Sasha touched Courtney on the arm. "When did you put yours on?"

Courtney tugged on a golden chain around her neck until a golden yellow charm rose from under her bodysuit. "Summer of '65. I was twenty-seven when we found it."

All of us tried to do the math in our heads, but it was no contest. "You're seventy-five years old?" Sasha shouted with surprise. "So, Camuto rounded up on your age?"

"No. Freaking. Way!" Selby was amazed, too. "You're *way* too hot to be that old."

I said the obvious. "Then gold ice *stops* you from aging?"

"Not quite," Courtney said, smirking. "Time for you three to get some sleep. Tomorrow's a big day for us all."

While Courtney gave us a tour the living quarters, I wondered how they made this living arrangement work – Hughes and two single women. Everyone used the same bathroom and showered in one area separated by a four-foot-high tiled wall. There were rows of bunk beds, but only four of them had sheets.

The girls showered first. Selby and I were told to wait in the bunk area. Together. Courtney had missed the cage match between Sasha and Rhapsody. Was she trying to start another one with us? I paced around, trying to avoid Selby. The room wasn't big enough for that. I ended up doing small circles, like a dog chasing his own tail.

"Quit it, Freshman," he said from a bottom bunk as I circled it. "You're making me nervous."

"Sorry," I said. What was I sorry for?

Lying back, he turned his head in my direction. "Think they ever hooked up? Moses and the Golden Girls? They had to, right?"

I was ashamed to admit I'd thought about it. "You mean Hughes and Courtney?"

He let out a chuckle. "*Hughes.* Dude's totally Janitor Brad. You knew that, right?"

"Yeah." At least someone else said it.

"It wouldn't be him and *Camuto.* Sour Lemon Face is totally a virgin."

I quickly changed the subject. "Why are you here? I thought you were leaving."

"Psssh. Sasha's right, you don't listen. I said *after tomorrow.*"

The idea Sasha talked to him was bothersome enough without her talking to him about *me*. What else had she told Selby about me? "Hear anything about your folks?"

The last time I asked him, he'd nearly killed me. This time, my chain was almost unbreakable. All he could do was stare. *"No,"* he said angrily. "Killer's still out there."

I didn't believe it. He'd once used his speed to run into the girls' locker room. What kept him from zipping into the police precinct and stealing information? He knew *something*. His dad had abused him. He might be happy he died, but his mom was gone, too. I didn't picture him letting go of their deaths that easy.

Selby scratched the stray hairs on his cheek. "They think it was a. . .what's the name for it? Serial killer. I think – yeah, that's it."

I didn't speak. He stopped talking for a moment. "Gutted alive. . ." His voice cracked.

Suddenly the sound of water skittering across the floor stopped. Sasha and Rhapsody were finished.

Selby got up from his bunk and tossed the white towel Courtney had given him over his shoulder. "It's about time. I'm first," he said.

With a *whoosh*, Selby sped out of the bunk room and into the showers. No more than thirty seconds later, he turned the water off. "All yours, *Freak.*"

I showered at a normal speed, but I kept an eye open for a sudden gust of wind. Now Selby could pull pranks at super-speed. It was bad enough we had to wear generic sets of clothes. At least they were close to our size. The underwear fit, too. I tried to not let that fact creep me out.

Returning to the bunks, I saw we all had chosen different sides of the room. Sasha had staked a claim to the top bunk closest to the lone window in the room. She looked up when she saw me, then turned her attention back to rubbing lotion on her arms. Rhapsody took the bottom bunk across the room from Sasha. She smiled at me, rolled her eyes at Sasha and continued brushing her hair. Selby wasn't around.

Rather than deal with either of them, I tracked my way back to the giant room and put my phone on one of their chargers. After searching for a while I found a flashlight by Hughes' desk. I could tell it was his desk by the giant liquor bottle next to one of its legs. It reminded me of Joyce's brandy. I picked it up by the neck and read the label. "*Oh*-ban single malt," I read. "What's the 'fourteen' mean?"

"It means it's fourteen-year-old whiskey. And it's pronounced 'Oh-*ben*'."

Hughes voice boomed from behind me. I jumped three feet into the air and got stuck. Gravity wasn't pulling me back to the floor, but I wasn't going any higher. I looked down and that's when my feet hit the ground with a *thud*.

He nodded like I had done something impressive. "Can't sleep?"

It was early, so maybe I could still sleep. "Not in there," I said.

"Follow me," he said, reaching into his drawer and producing two lowball glasses. "Bring the flashlight and the bottle."

I stared at him. I'd never drunk alcohol before. "You know I'm fifteen, right?"

"Trust me," he laughed. "Underage drinking is the least of your problems."

He had a point. I did what he told me to do.

Hughes directed me to the elevator, and we got inside. "Push the 'T' button."

I did it. The elevator brought us to the second level – the one I'd been curious about. I flicked the flashlight on and shined it ahead of us. Sure enough, those mammoth shadows were jet airplanes. I had seen photos of planes like these in my history book. We passed them all and another machine I couldn't even begin to describe beyond its distinctive shape – like a giant metal needle with a control panel.

By flipping a few nearby switches, Hughes turned on the lights. He sat with his back against the giant needle and instructed me to do the same. I handed him the bottle and he poured himself some whiskey, then some for me.

"I don't toast to other men," he said, drinking it in one gulp. "Drink up."

I sniffed it first. Whiskey smells horrible and strong, like funky cologne. "If I pour this in one of them," I said, pointing my left hand toward the planes, "will it start?"

Hughes cracked a smile and poured himself some more. "Funny. Don't sip it. Your body will process it quickly enough."

"My therapist says I shouldn't drink because of my rage blackouts."

He said the word loudly enough for his voice to echo. "Thera-pist? Thera-pist?"

"Well played."

"I'll take personal responsibility for you, Rage Against the Machine. Drink up."

I hate nicknames.

Holding my breath, I sucked it down. It tasted sweet for a split second and then worse than I ever imagined it would. Instead of spitting it out, I swallowed it. "This tastes good to you?" I asked, coughing.

"Yeah," he said after his second glass. "You'll get used to it."

Drinking underage wasn't the first law I'd broken, but it was almost the least satisfying – right after breaking into Peters' house and getting shot. "I doubt it."

"Since you're one of us," he said, pouring himself a little less this time. "The rules and laws of regular people don't really apply to you anymore. You have to adapt, set your own evolving sense of right and wrong."

"Is that what happened to King?"

Hughes noticeably flinched, drinking some of the whiskey before setting his glass next to him on the concrete. "Your ways of thinking about things have to constantly change, Jason. Long life has its benefits and its consequences. That's what happened to King."

Though that didn't make much sense, I belched before I could control it. "You can't take your necklace off, can you?"

"Drink some more, Kid," he said, measuring whiskey into my glass.

This time I quickly swallowed the liquid, letting it burn its way down my throat and into my stomach. The sweetness lingered on my tongue a little longer this time. I blinked in slow motion, or did I?

"We've lived so long," he said with a hint of sadness in his voice. "So long."

I asked him. "King wants the provenance crystals. Why? They're going to blow up."

Hughes gazed into his glass, like Joyce had done the last time I saw her. But while Joyce looked as if she wished the glass was bigger, his face grew dark and regretful. "A long time ago he started wearing a pink prism. Ever since then, David's been. . .rather psychotic."

Psychotic. He'd said it casually, like if I asked what color King's hair color was. That didn't explain what he wanted with it, but maybe Hughes didn't know himself. "How am I supposed to find the blue and gold ones?"

He stifled a belch in his throat and poured me a bit more. "Very carefully."

I drank the whiskey without thinking. *Are my lips numb?* "Howww?"

"You reach down inside yourself, past your fears, and do it. You're more capable than you know."

Suddenly my eyelids felt impossible to keep open. I put my hands down on the floor to steady the spinning in my head. The alcohol churned in my stomach, and I hoped it stayed there. "You owe me. . .fifty bucksss. . .*Brad.*"

I saw three of Hughes in front of me, and they all smiled. "You just drank it. Good night."

CHAPTER FIFTEEN

off to the mountains

The next thing I remembered was waking up across from Sasha's bunk. She wasn't in it. Rhapsody was gone, too. Selby's bunk hadn't been slept in at all.

Last night Hughes and I had drunk a lot of expensive whiskey. I'd never had a hangover, so what was I supposed to feel? A headache? Throwing up? The inside of my mouth was like cotton, but that was normal for me when my powers were active.

My thoughts were all over the place, but that wasn't unusual, either. I needed my Adderall. Courtney was right. The prisms sped up everything our bodies did, including flushing out alcohol. I didn't have a hangover.

I washed up, put on my bodysuit over my clothes, and unzipped it down to the middle of my chest. Letting the arms hang, I walked through the hallways, the giant round room, and into the dining room. Everyone had eaten, except for me. Sasha was still at the table, stabbing her fork in her eggs.

"Hey," she said when I arrived. "Go eat. Hughes is cleaning up now."

I ducked my head into the kitchen. "You owe me fifty bucks, *Brad.*"

In the midst of washing dishes, Hughes turned off the faucet and let out a rolling laugh. "You drank it last night, *Captain.*"

Sasha spit out some of her orange juice. "You *drank* alcohol with Hughes?"

I got a paper plate and plastic utensils from the table. "I'm starving."

"That's *not* an answer," Sasha said as I served myself. "My mother's an alcoholic, Jason. Could you be a little more considerate?"

Popping two sausage links into my mouth, I mumbled an insincere "sorry." Though I stuffed myself, it didn't take long for me to eat. Courtney said that when I finished I should meet them in the "control room." *I guess that's the big round room.*

That's where I found everyone – our three guardians, Sasha, and Rhapsody. Once we were all present, Selby zoomed in from wherever he had been.

Hughes used a remote control to unfold a glass screen from the ceiling. The mechanism was huge, like a see-through movie screen. It descended and set up at the center of the control room.

The seven of us crowded into a semicircle around it. The screen powered on and displayed a three-dimensional map of North America with three colored blinking lights on it – one red, one green, and one white. All were far apart.

"What are the Christmas lights about?" Selby asked them.

My heart and brain raced. I couldn't think or speak. They knew where I'd hidden the crystals.

Camuto pointed to each colored dot. The green was in Montana, the red in Colorado and the white in Mexico. "These are the locations of the source crystals we know about, besides the pink."

Selby turned and shouted in my face. "Seriously, *Freak?* I thought you hid them. Man, *you* suck at this!"

"I move them around all of the time!" I yelled back. "It's not my fault."

Courtney laid a hand on my arm. "We're familiar with their radioactive signatures. There's no way you could have hidden them from us without help."

I watched Sasha's expression change. She was *thinking.*

"Whatever," I said.

"Does that mean somebody else knows where they are?" Rhapsody asked.

"Yes," Camuto said it like we should have known that already. "We don't have a lot of time left to explain fine details. It'll only get worse if we wait any longer."

Great. "Do we have any kind of advantage here?" I asked.

Courtney, Camuto, and Hughes all looked at me. "You can lift and move them by yourself," Camuto said. "It will take him much longer."

"Do you have any white ice here?" Sasha asked. "Even red ice would help. Running into problems would be a lot less of an issue if we could take their powers away or. . .mind control our enemies."

Her hesitation in saying "mind control" let me know she thought about what she had done to Officer Spivey.

"Not an option," Hughes said. "We don't keep any isotopes in house."

"Why not?" Selby wondered aloud. "What if someone attacked *you?*"

"Go and get the green one first," Courtney said, brushing off his question. She pointed to the glowing emerald dot. "Montana is closest. Mexico is last. We have weak leads on the locations of the blue and gold. Those will take the longest to find."

Rhapsody fanned her hands. "Wait, why are we going to Mexico *last?* They're using white ice in weapons. Won't King or whoever want that one before the others?"

"Yeah, psychopath with weapons," Selby said. "I vote no."

Sasha pointed at the map. "They have a point. We should shift strategy."

Hands on hips, Courtney said, "You need the *green and red* prisms for fighting back. We've been at this for a long time, guys. Give me a little credit here on this one."

"If we get the white first, there *is* no fight," Sasha argued. "And truth? The 'we're-really-old-and-experienced' argument is a little ridiculous."

"Enough," I shouted, clapping my hands. "Green one first, okay?"

"Who died and made you intelligent?" Selby asked me.

I wanted to say "your momma," but she had been murdered. "I'm the captain."

Selby threw up his hands. "Fine, *Captain*. I'm in the wind at midnight."

Together we moved over to Camuto's desk. On top of it sat Courtney's shiny briefcase, the one from Rhapsody's house. After a fingerprint scan, she opened it and plucked three small squares and four watches from the gray felt inside.

"Replace your cell phone SIM cards," she said, handing new chips to Sasha, Rhapsody, and Selby. "Jason, I already changed yours while it was charging overnight on Hughes' desk. The police can't track you with these. Neither can King. At the height of the storm, they will still explode, so you will have to ditch them."

Debra would be glad I was finally off of her wireless plan. "Thanks," I said while they went to work on their phones. "What are *those?*" I pointed to the watches.

"Miniature Geiger counters," Camuto said as Courtney gave me one. "They're tuned to the high proton energy radiation of the source crystals. When you get close, it'll start clicking. The faster the click, the closer the proximity to a provenance crystal."

"Alright," Selby said. He reassembled his phone and strapped the watch to his wrist. "What are we waiting for here, an invitation?"

Rhapsody waved her hand. "Question. Can I make a quick call?"

Hughes nodded. "You'll have to make it fast. Your signal will work now that you're on our system."

Camuto had lied, but I didn't care at this point. Maybe she had to clear it with the others, or someone had to be present when we called.

Rhapsody crossed over to the other side of the room, I guessed, to call Ruby. I did the same and picked up my phone from Hughes' desk to phone Debra. The phone rang once and my stepmother picked up.

"Hello?" she asked. She sounded agitated. "Hello? Who is this?"

I faced Sasha and Selby, who were standing around and waiting for us. At that second it occurred to me – neither of them had anyone to call. "It's me, Debra. . ."

She interrupted me before I could identify myself. "Who are you looking for, Ma'am?"

Ma'am? I doubted that I sounded like a woman, but I played along. "I'm going away for a while, you know, to save the world or something like that. How are you?"

"Fine. I understand. But you've still got the wrong number, I'm sure."

"I'll be back when I can. Give my brother a hug for me. I love. . ."

"I'm sorry, but nobody by that name lives here," she said before hanging up.

I didn't quite understand what happened, but I tried to absorb it. Debra was talking in code. *She's in trouble. I wish I could find out how much right now.*

Rhapsody finished her call and looked every bit as confused as I was. "Ready?"

"Yeah," I said, hoping my family was alright. "Did you call Ruby?"

Rhapsody exhaled frustration as we walked back over to the group. "I think so." She talked so quickly I could barely understand what she was saying."

Hughes interrupted us. "Jason with Rhapsody, Michael with Sasha. Stay invisible in the air. Both of you

– keep your speed transonic or lower. Any faster and you could kill the girls or lose them in transit."

Wait, Selby can move as fast as I can jump?

"I can handle *that,*" Selby said, eyeing Sasha like he could see through her bodysuit.

His speed was the only thing keeping me from throwing him through the ceiling. "Knock it off, Leslie. We're out."

"Good luck," Courtney said as we left the control room. "Dial star on your phones to check in."

The four of us boarded the elevator. Sasha pressed her face into my shoulder and closed her eyes.

"What's her deal?" Selby pointed his thumb at her.

"Claustrophobia," I reminded him. He, of all people, shouldn't have forgotten.

I pressed the unmarked button and we eventually reached the surface level. The entryway opened up to the field of weeds. Silent, we walked out in a line. Sasha started breathing normally again. The eleven o'clock sun was at full strength overhead with no clouds to shield it.

"We're going northeast to the green source first," I said, tracking our direction by the sun and turning in a half circle. "I'll guide you in. I'm pretty sure that's *this* way."

Sasha pointed me a few degrees to my left and tapped her wrist. "You were close. There's a compass on this watch they gave us."

Rhapsody sidled next to me. "Alright. Saddle up and let's get it."

"Uh uh," Sasha said, wagging her finger. "I don't care which crystal we go after first or what Camuto said. I'm going with *my boyfriend*. You go with Selby."

Selby stepped in. "Nah. He can carry her, Sasha, no problem – he's super-strong. You're built better for wind resistance anyway."

Rhapsody turned pale at his comment. "Screw yourself, Selby, and you know what? When you do, I bet it'll last longer than your sex tape did."

Selby's face flushed bright red. He picked up Sasha around the waist and left a cloud of weeds and dirt behind them.

Rhapsody and I donned our masks and jumped. I stayed on a high arc and she turned us invisible. We were going so fast that she didn't move much in my arms. She might have been afraid I'd drop her, but I'd never let that happen.

About half past twelve we touched down in a dusty Montana valley. I'd buried the green provenance crystal in the side of a mountain. The peaks were high and rocky brown. Our masks fed us a steady supply of oxygen, so we kept them on our faces. The altitude made it difficult to breathe. In the distance we heard a wolverine howling. The first time I was here, the echo of their hungry growling had creeped me out. Rhapsody shivered, so it had the same effect on her.

Above us was the hole. I'd piled rocks in front of it. Our watches were rapidly clicking now, like the second hand of an enormous clock.

"Where do you think Selby and Sasha are?" I asked slightly worried.

"Maybe he couldn't run over the mountains at a high speed?" Rhapsody asked through her mask. "It's not like there's a bike trail around here."

That was part of the reason I'd chosen to hide it here. "I'll go get it. Can you call them?"

Rhapsody unmasked. "Yeah. I'll hit up Selby," she said.

Hopping up to an area of rock large enough to support my weight, I wound up and sent a punch into the rock pile. I tossed the largest stone away and looked inside. A bright emerald glow greeted me. I sighed and dug ahead. "It's still here," I called down to Rhapsody.

"Good," she shouted up to me. "Hurry. I don't have a good feeling right now."

I unearthed the source crystal. Shaped like an oversized letter-T, it had grown a full set of prisms since the last time I'd moved it. I put it across my shoulders and jumped back down to where Rhapsody stood. "What's wrong?" I asked her.

"Selby's not answering," she said. "Neither is Sasha."

CHAPTER SIXTEEN

trouble and pizza

When I laid the source crystal down next to us the ground trembled a little. Slipping my hand into my bodysuit, I located my phone and punched star. Instead of ringing, it did this awkward-sounding set of high-toned beeps.

Camuto picked up. "Make the delivery and proceed to location two."

Her aloofness caught me off-guard. "We've got the green," I said through my mask. "Sasha and Selby are missing."

"No, *they're not.*" Camuto's anger played out well over the phone. "They're halfway to location three."

Mexico? *I should have known – Camuto and the others are tracking us.* "They went without us?" I said loudly enough for Rhapsody to hear.

She rolled her eyes. "To the white source? That doesn't even make sense. Who's going to move it?"

I had my doubts about Sasha's choice in boys, outside of me, of course, but I never questioned her intelligence. If it was her idea to go there, she had a good reason.

"Green and red are the *priority,*" Camuto insisted. "Bring it back and head to location two."

The sharpness in her voice was getting on my nerves, so I hung up the phone. We were much closer to Colorado from here than we would be from the base.

"How far out are we from them?" Rhapsody asked.

I tried to calculate the distance in my head. "It's. . .I don't know, two hours? It would take us almost an hour-and-a-half to go back."

"What if you up your speed – faster than they said you should go?"

How fast was above transonic? "I've never tried."

She touched my arm with her gloved hand. "Put it back into the cave. I'll stay."

"No," I shook my head. "Way too dangerous. I'll put it back and you leave with me. If King's coming here, he'll find it and you alone. He'll *kill* you."

"On the real? We can't risk leaving it here, either. What about Sasha and Selby?"

Maybe we should do what Camuto told us to do, after all. I lifted the source crystal and heaved it over my right shoulder. "Come here, please," I told her.

Rhapsody moved to my left and wrapped her arms around my neck. I grabbed her tightly and leaped for the underground fortress.

When we landed, I could barely wait for the entryway to open, so Rhapsody ghosted us down to the basement level. We rushed to meet Courtney, Camuto, and Hughes in the room where they stored the pink source. Only Camuto and Hughes were there.

I set it in the hole to the far right and unmasked. "We abandoned our friends for your 'mission'," I said. "Here's your crystal. I'm going to Mexico."

"W-w-wait!" Hughes yelled. "Stick to the plan. You've got to hit location two."

A vein in my neck pulsed with the anger boiling in my brain. "*You* hit 'location two'," I shouted. "What are you doing down here while we risk our lives, anyway?"

"Monitoring detail, in case one of you does something stupid, like going to the wrong location," Hughes said to me. "Sasha and Selby can protect themselves."

Camuto's eyes narrowed. "Can they, Solomon? I hate to admit it, but none of this would've happened if we had trusted them in the first place."

"*Trusted them?* They went against orders, Amauri." Hughes was fuming. "They're *children.* They're not worthy of our trust."

Rhapsody waved her hand, pointing to us. "Hello? Standing right here. . ."

". . .whatever happens – it's not on our heads. I'm not leaving the future of humanity in the hands of four children, even if you and Eris are."

"I'm a child who can knock the teeth out of your mouth, *Brad,*" I said.

While we argued and cursed at each other, Rhapsody stepped away. She whipped out her phone and dialed. Holding it to her ear she paced, stopping to redial.

"Neither of them is answering," she yelled over the noise.

Camuto stopped us from talking. "Michael can't stop on a dime to answer your call, Rhapsody," she said with regret. "He'll have to gradually decrease his speed and slow down to a normal run."

"This is all we do," Hughes said. "If either of you goes to Mexico now, you could be risking everything for nothing."

I stood so close to Hughes that I heard him breathing. "Sasha and Selby aren't *nothing*," I said, my teeth clenched. "You said you don't keep ice down here?"

"No," he admitted. He was wondering what I was thinking.

"Then help us and don't try to stop me."

I stormed off. Rhapsody followed close on my heels. "Jason, wait!" she said, hopping into the elevator before I closed the wire mesh gate.

Pressing the unmarked button, I turned away from her. "I'm going alone."

The elevator rattled and started going up. "No, you're *not*," she argued. "They're my friends, too."

"I can get there faster by myself."

"Yeah, but I'll keep you off the grid," she said. Her eyes flitted back and forth. "Eventually the military will figure out how to track you if you keep taking risks."

We arrived at the top level. "I'll take my chances."

We stood in the dark. Rhapsody was within arms' reach. She moved closer. My heart thumped hard in my chest. I smelled the faint scent of her flowery perfume.

"Even if you don't need me," she said, her voice trembling. "I need *you*."

There, in suffocating silence, I listened to Rhapsody pour out her soul to me.

"I just said goodbye to my dad. Ruby is. . .I don't know if she's safe or not. I'm not losing you, too, Jason. So I'm going, whether you like it or not."

Are they going to open this thing or do I have to punch through it? "Alright," I said.

"Good." Her voice bounced with enthusiasm.

We must have gotten to Hughes or Camuto – the gears of the fortress's opening turned and whirred. Soon afterward we walked outside and departed for Mexico.

We needed to make a pit stop on the pier. By the time we reached San Diego, it was close to four. Stopping at a pizza place, we pretended to be extras from a movie set to excuse the bodysuits. Apparently there was a nearby costume play event going on soon, so we fit in.

Eating was the last thing on our minds, but both of us were on the verge of passing out from using our powers so much. It amazed me that my medicine hadn't worn off yet. We unzipped our suits to the waist, sat in the sand beneath the pier, and leaned against one of its weight-bearing beams. We'd inhale our pizza slices and soda in five minutes and make up the time in the air.

After saying a quick prayer, I dug in. Rhapsody did her sign of the cross and started eating. I couldn't help thinking about Sasha. Was she in trouble? My chewing slowed. What if we got there too late? Would King do to them what we thought he'd done to Selby's parents and Asia?

Suddenly I wasn't as hungry anymore.

Rhapsody slurped her drink. "Mmm, what's up? You thinking about them?"

"Is it that obvious?"

She nodded. "From the way you look, you're either worried or constipated. I'm hoping it's worry. Otherwise, you probably shouldn't be eating so much cheese."

A small laugh escaped me. I looked down at the slice and a half I had left and my almost full cup of Sprite. A salty mid-afternoon breeze blew in from over the water. The water came in small waves, wetting the sand just feet in front of us.

Rhapsody took a bite of pizza. "Look," she said, wiping her hands on a napkin. "Everything we've been through since we got these crystals – we've done things, taken chances no ordinary person would."

"Right," I said, absentmindedly biting into one of my slices.

"There's no game plan here. Nobody's been down this road. Yeah, we make mistakes, but the people saying 'wrong, wrong' are doing nothing but watching us."

She had a point. I ate some more and took a sip of Sprite. "Why do you think they told us to go to Montana first? Isn't Mexico closer?"

"I'm Panamanian, dude. Beats me. Geography isn't my bag."

With my appetite back, I ate fast and finished my soda. "Ready?" I asked her minutes later.

"Almost," she said, shoving a crust into her mouth. "Gotta pee."

Rhapsody made a bee line for the blue and white portable toilet stations. I did the same. Unfortunately there was nowhere to wash my hands. When I finished, I got close enough to the tide to dip my hands into the cold salt water. Satisfied, I shook my hands dry and got back into my suit. To my right, I saw Rhapsody doing the same thing. We shared a laugh. I appreciated a momentary break in the tension.

CHAPTER SEVENTEEN

we meet a King

When hiding a nuclear bomb made of crystal, you want to make it tough to find. It can't be underground, which is where the prisms grow. That doesn't leave a lot of options. With the white one I found the perfect spot in Mexico – a volcano. *It sounds crazy when I say it out loud.* A volcanic explosion wouldn't kill me, and the threat of boiling lava narrowed the field of who could get to the provenance crystal.

Rhapsody left us invisible until the second our feet touched near the volcano's base close to seven p.m. Turned out, she didn't need to. A hazy wet mist was blowing in hard from the west. The storm cloaked our appearance but also made it nearly impossible for us to see. Using our hands, we cleared the moisture from the dark eye plates in our masks. Of all the things these bodysuits had, wipers weren't one of them.

"How are we going to find them in this?" Rhapsody screamed in my ear.

I had no idea. Instead, I pointed up and then to my wrist. Though we couldn't hear it, the Geiger counter was clicking at a rapid clip. The crystal was *close*.

Punching and kicking through the surface rock, I created spots for Rhapsody to hold onto. As long as she stayed close behind me, she'd see them. The slippery climb was treacherous because of the crappy weather. I compensated for the slick surface by adjusting my grip, but Rhapsody had no choice but to do it the regular way.

After she lost her hold once and nearly fell, I stopped and dangled my foot. She grabbed it and pulled herself up onto me. With Rhapsody clinging tightly to my back, I continued climbing.

Together, we made it to the shelf of black rock I'd created. Like I had done to the mountain in Montana, I burrowed my hand deep into the rock and pulled out debris until the hole became visible. A burst of white light flashed through the space.

Rhapsody released me and stepped onto the stony platform. "Nice hiding spot."

"This one I didn't plan to move for a while," I said.

We hunched over in the narrow corridor and moved closer. My insides lurched. Were we alone? I reached for Rhapsody's hand and squeezed it. We vanished.

Then I noticed my fingers fading back into view. Panicked, I looked around but didn't see anyone. There had to be someone using them against her. The white source was a remote control to turn powers off. Someone had to be pushing the button.

Pain blasted through my body. I cursed in agony. My right knee buckled and I crumpled into a pile onto the makeshift cave's floor. I could barely breathe, much less string together a thought. "Rhap. . ." I said, reaching my hand out to my friend. My eyesight blurred, but one thing I was sure of.

Someone was behind her.

I opened my right eye. The left side of my face was smashed against a tile floor. I tugged at my hands – they were bound together by something hard. A small circle of pink moisture pooled on the floor in front of my mouth. *Where am I? Mexico?*

Groaning, I curled into a ball and tucked my legs through my arms. Rolling to a sitting position let me get a good view of the place I was being held. The walls were beige with a stucco texture. I sniffed the scent of burning oil from a lamp lighting the darkened room. My bad lung ached. The knee pain was halfway tolerable if I didn't move it.

Squinting in its faint yellow light, I waited until my eyes adjusted. There were four people in here with me. Sasha slumped against one corner. Selby had been propped up against one, too. Rhapsody slept in the closest corner to me. Someone else lay face down next to me in a pair of shorts and a dark-colored t-shirt.

I scooted over to see the back of his head. Ryan Cain. I thought he worked for King, not against him?

Everyone but me was unconscious.

I positioned myself against the wall with the lamp. Calling out each of their names in a whisper, I expected someone to respond. None of them moved except to breathe. At least I knew they were alive.

Sometime later I drifted off, occasionally waking up when the tightness in my chest got to be too much. Before now I hadn't been tired, even after traveling thousands of miles. I slept because my injuries or something else was forcing me to do so. We had been drugged or mind-controlled – maybe both?

The world spun around me. I passed out again.

Cold water splashed across my face.

"¡Buenas tardes," said a rough-looking American man holding a silver metal pitcher in front of me. Dressed in green fatigues, he had a military buzz cut. His beard was grizzled black and gray over his square cheeks and jaw. He smelled of tobacco and strong coffee.

Good afternoon – it was Sunday? I fought the urge to stick out my dry tongue to cool it off. He poured some into a small white cup and held it at my lips, nodding to indicate I should drink it. "¿No tienes sed," he asked.

"He's asking if you're thirsty," Rhapsody said, exhausted. "Don't drink it."

The man shouted at Rhapsody in Spanish before pressing his fist against my chest. When I moaned in torment, he poured the water into my mouth and held it and my nose shut until I was forced to swallow it. Drugged or not, it was cold, wet, and wonderful.

Satisfied, he backed away and spoke to someone on the other side of the door. I expected a bunch of Mexican officers to rush in. Instead, kids our age rushed into the cell. Two Hispanic boys put their hands under my arms to drag me out. A red-haired Caucasian girl with toned arms and a dark-skinned Indian boy lifted Ryan and carried him behind me. The others weren't far behind.

"Help us," I mumbled to my captors. "Crystals. . .they're going to explode."

"They already know *that*," the man who gave me water said in plain English as they pulled me forward. "Unlike the Collective, *we're* not trying to stop it."

The boys took me to the back of a large truck with a cloth cover. Pulling it aside, they set me on a bench and strapped me in. I waited for the others. Selby was placed to my right and Ryan at my left. Across from us were Sasha and Rhapsody. Sasha had a bruised bottom lip and a nasty scrape on her right cheek. Rhapsody was fine.

"Was that. . .*King?*" I managed. Breathing without pain was a challenge.

"It wasn't Kanye West," Ryan said. "Yes, it was King."

Selby winced. I tried not to smile – he had broken ribs, courtesy of my hitting him with a lead pipe months ago. He hadn't healed, either.

"King caught us at the Orizaba city limits," Sasha said, favoring the right side of her mouth. "Shut off Selby's speed all at once. Stopping was. . .painful."

"We were climbing when he grabbed us," Rhapsody said.

Ryan looked at Rhapsody and then at me. "Yeah, you were."

"Why are you even here?" I blurted out all in one labored breath. When my strength returned, I owed him one for stabbing my stepmother.

The exhaust pipe of the truck coughed out a cloud of black smoke. The undercarriage produced a tinny rattle and the vehicle moved forward at a slow speed. I propped my leg out for leverage, forgetting I had torn knee ligaments. Only the seat belt kept me in place. I cursed and dragged it back next to my other one.

"Yeah, why *are* you here, Cain? Weren't you working *for* King?" Selby asked.

Ryan rolled his neck and stared at Selby. "Don't know if you overheard, but his big plan is to let those things blow. He's going to absorb the radiation himself and. . ."

Rhapsody's eyes bulged. "If that isn't the craziest, most batsh--"

". . .he thinks it will make him *immortal* or something," Ryan finished. "The kids who have powers are helping him. He goes inside our minds whenever he wants. When he read mine and found out I wasn't down with it, I became like one of you to him."

"Absorbing high proton radiation will make him *immortal?*" Sasha restated it as a question she was asking herself. She gazed at the cloth and metal roof of the truck. "Either he's right or he'll melt like butter and the world will be a continent short."

Rhapsody bit her bottom lip. "How do we *stop it?*"

"I've got an idea," Ryan said.

"If we knew how to stop him," Sasha sneered at Rhapsody. "We wouldn't. . ."

"I'm *so sorry*, Sasha," Rhapsody interrupted. "Can't understand your idea. Lift your butt a little higher so we can all hear you talking out of it."

While the girls sniped back and forth with each other and Selby tried stopping them from arguing, Ryan elbowed me in the arm. "Did you see the hot redhead in there? The one that picked me up?" he asked.

"Yeah," I said, wondering where he was going with this.

"She's from back home. Went to North, too. I've been smashing her for a month."

Why is this fool telling me about his sex life in the middle of a crisis? I stretched my sore neck. "You must not be any good at it," I said, gasping. "She put you in here."

He glared at me. "It's an *act*, Champion. She had to make it convincing."

I let the jokes go and heard him out. "Congrats. How are. . .you going to get us out of here?"

He shook his head no. "I'm not. *You are.*"

Ryan turned his body toward me, revealing a green prism in his palms. Carefully, without touching him, I plucked the crystal from his hand. Instantly my body returned to normal. I broke the plastic bands around my wrists and stood up.

That got Rhapsody and Sasha's attention away from each other. I freed Ryan and then Selby, with the girls last.

"Pop an Adderall and get us out of here," Rhapsody said.

I unzipped my suit and fished around the pocket over my heart. King had taken my supply, along with my phone and Geiger counter. "I'm out."

Sasha wrapped her hand around the inside of her bodysuit. "No worries. When Hughes and Camuto came for me, I grabbed some. It's what a good girlfriend does."

She handed me a pill and I swallowed it, hoping the little bit of spit in my mouth was enough for it to go down. "Ryan, where did they take our stuff? We need it."

He wagged his index finger. "I don't hate you enough to send you there. But there's somewhere else we can go."

"Alright," Sasha said. "Rhapsody, can you ghost all of us out of here?"

I handed the crystal over to Rhapsody. Leaning on Selby and Ryan for support, I braced for the worst as we all slowly passed through the bottom of the moving truck.

CHAPTER EIGHTEEN

a suicide mission

Ducking into an alley between a bakery and a clothing store, the five of us watched the truck motor off in the dust without us. Sooner or later King would figure out we had escaped. He was part of the Collective once, so he might have their tracking technology. Meaning the fact I had a green crystal made me a moving target. Good thing I could move pretty fast.

Selby, however, was in bad shape. "Ryan." My stomach tensed. "Selby can't go on like this. He needs a crystal."

"I'm aware of that," Ryan said, clenching his jaw. "It's a suicide mission."

"We don't have a choice, do we, Sasha?" Rhapsody asked.

"No." She looked down. The two of them had formed a truce. Or, at least they had agreed to stop bothering each other long enough for us to figure this out.

Ryan crossed his arms in front of his chest. "There's a one-level base north of here in Tamaulipas. If he has any prisms worth the trouble, they're there."

I tilted my head. "What if I got Rhapsody there and she ghosted through?"

Sasha looked away. "It *could* work."

Selby tightened his fists. "Why risk *two* people? I can zip in and be out faster."

"They'll see you coming," Ryan said, scratching his right eyebrow. "Champion's right. He and Rhapsody give us the best chance of getting out of here."

"Well, what about you?" I asked him. "I mean, I can carry you. But without a bodysuit, it'll take forever to get home."

"Just get me a red crystal. I'll even take gold," Ryan said, stepping back. "I can handle myself. We'll be here when you get back."

Rhapsody pulled her mask down and waited for me to do the same. I put the green crystal in my bodysuit's inside pocket. Leaning over to Sasha's left, I kissed her on the cheek. "I'll be back for you," I said in her ear before putting my mask on.

She stared past me into the distance. "You'd better."

We closed in on our location. I felt it. Debra said the deep down place was my spirit, not my stomach. I wasn't sure what it was, but it hadn't led me wrong yet.

Rhapsody never moved much in the air, but her hand drifted from my neck to right over my heart. Warmth flowed through my veins and I started sweating. What was she doing? Then I realized she needed to use the crystal to turn us invisible.

We descended behind the metal fence around the compound. Dressed in all-black uniforms, two kids a little older than we were guarded the entrance. They had machine guns leaning against their shoulders. White ice weapons.

"Can you levitate us in?" she whispered. "It's just – they'll see your footprints."

I thought back to the time in the control room, when I jumped and stopped in the air. "Hughes told you I could do that?" I asked her in a quiet voice.

"He told everyone. Just try it. I couldn't turn intangible until I had to, remember?"

I didn't have to come up with something to make me afraid, like I had been in the control room. Things were getting out of control and fast.

Rather than use my whole foot to jump, I pushed off on my toes. We rocketed straight up into the air, almost as high as the knob on the flagpole and remained there.

Rhapsody wiggled a little bit and held onto me tighter. I could tell she was looking straight down.

"Umm. . .let's get down, Cap. *Slowly.*"

Dialing down our altitude, I focused on the flat roof of the building. Gradually we drifted over it. Neither of us said anything, in case it was a fluke. It wasn't. Focusing on slow moving things helped me put on the brakes. Molasses, old people crossing the street, ants. It was working!

At just the right moment Rhapsody ghosted us through the building. The place looked a little bit like the Collective's fortress. Actually, it was designed *a lot* like it. Instead of gray metal, the beams and walls were navy blue. The feel of the building was newer and modernized with more up-to-date technology. There were card sensors by each door and televisions on the walls that doubled as electronic billboards. Had the Mexican military built this place, or had King done it himself?

Rhapsody and I solidified on the bottom floor, where many of the teenage soldiers milled about. Among them I saw Ryan's girlfriend but didn't get a good look at her face. All of them were wearing *gold* prism necklaces. No red or green. *Great! Something else to worry about.*

King emerged from a brightly-lit room adjacent to where we stood. The white source must be in there. Sasha was right again. He went after it first and laid a trap for those of us who came after it.

He walked straight over to a black glass table. On its face was an interactive map of the world. It looked *exactly* like the one belonging to Camuto and Hughes.

Rhapsody and I stood close enough to see the display. A solid white dot blinked near the coast in Mexico. The red dot in Colorado was solid, too, while Montana had a blinking green dot. If solid means it's missing, who had gotten to the red source before we did?

"Did you give him a green isotope like I asked?" King said over his shoulder.

The redheaded girl turned her head to face him. "I did."

I cursed in my head. She'd been playing Ryan all of this time. Figures he'd be that stupid.

King swiped his palms over the glass surface. A different map appeared, one with miniature people on it. There was a cluster of gold people in Mexico and one, lone, green person in the middle of them.

Me.

King looked around the room and waved his left hand. On its fourth finger was a ring made entirely of white ice. "Ryan? Where are you? No? Maybe one of our other friends. . ."

I wheeled around and snatched the gold prism necklaces off of every kid around me. Something strange happened to them when I did. Immediately their bodies turned a dark shade of brown and withered up, like dry leaves in the sun.

"Go!" Rhapsody shouted.

With her in my arms, I jumped out of the basement. We fell into a bare room on the middle floor. I'd never stopped in the middle of a jump before. The green prism tumbled from my fist when I hit the ground. It was clear. How had that happened?

Rhapsody pounded the floor with her fist. She had lost her power, too.

My body started aching again. "What the. . .?"

Right then a brassy siren blared throughout the building. Visible and vulnerable, we looked at each other with alarm.

"Quick! Give me one," she said.

I tossed her a gold prism necklace and tied one around my own neck. My knee and lungs were fine again! We didn't have time to test what else it could do, but I hoped my strength and her intangibility were included. Shoving the remainder of the prisms into my suit, I picked up Rhapsody and jumped in no particular direction.

We passed through the building at blinding speed, way faster than I had intended to go, than I had ever gone. I tightened my grasp on Rhapsody but after a long time in the sky, I felt her slipping. At this speed, I couldn't see clearly, so I thought to slow down just enough to see how far we had gone.

I blinked to make sure I was seeing correctly. Orizaba was directly below us, with the alley we had been hiding in not much farther.

I was too nervous to drop in between two buildings, so we landed on the sidewalk of a busy street. Once we had unmasked, Rhapsody let our invisibility down.

She put her hand on her chest. "My God, that was amazing! Do you feel different?"

The energy of the gold crystal was higher than the green – like the difference between licking a double AA battery and a car battery. "Definitely," I said.

Rhapsody squealed and gave me a lingering touch on the arm. "It's incredible. I mean, my whole body's tingling. I've *never* felt this good before."

Her eyes were glassy. Things were getting a little weird again. "We should go."

"No, wait, Jason. I need to say this while I can." Rhapsody made eye contact with me. "Sasha and I go at it like we do because. . .well, I really like you and she knows it."

The hairs on the back of my neck stood at attention. "R-rhapsody, I. . ."

"I know you're with her right now," she said, her smile building slowly. "I didn't say anything all this time because. . .I thought you. . .couldn't be into a Goth. We're way different. But I think, deep down, you like me, too. And we could be *beautiful* together."

Listening to her, I gained a presence of our surroundings. People were walking past us, staring, especially at Rhapsody. I heard children speaking to their parents and the sound of moving vehicles. The scent of fresh bread wafted through the air. We were standing in front of a bakery. My armpits were sweating inside my suit, even though the cooling apparatus was on.

I didn't want to say yes to Rhapsody, but I couldn't say no.

"We've had some close calls," she said, taking the pressure off of me to speak. Her lip trembled. "I don't want to die. But if I do, it's no regrets."

I can respect that," I finally managed to say. We left it there.

Selby, Sasha, and Ryan were waiting for us in the alleyway. Sasha flung herself into my arms and kissed me, despite her hurt lip. A pang of guilt hit me inside, but I returned the kiss.

"That was quick," she said, slowly backing away from me.

With my back to the street, I unzipped my suit enough to free the crystals. I tossed one to Rhapsody, then Sasha and Selby.

"Righteous!" Selby yelled after he tied his necklace. "Thanks, Freak."

I saved Ryan for last. Channeling all of my natural strength, I popped Ryan in the nose with my right fist. He immediately started bleeding.

"That's for Julia," I said, tossing a necklace at his feet. "We're not close to even."

Ryan pinched his nose. "How did you get these?" he asked in a nasal voice.

"Stole them," I said, proud of myself. "Why? What's the problem?"

"There's a list of what these things can do," Ryan said. He tied his necklace around his wrist as a bracelet. Blood continued running down his face, which he wiped off with the back of his hand. "What I learned. . .the real thing you need to know."

"Spit it out, dude," Selby said.

Ryan licked his bottom lip. "With heliodor, some of your powers will work very well. Others won't work at all."

CHAPTER NINETEEN

more powers, more problems

Ryan did his best to explain the situation with the gold crystals, but we kept interrupting him with a slew of questions.

Selby stopped cursing long enough to ask the most important one. "What does that mean, 'our powers won't work'?"

Ryan drew a deep breath and exhaled. "As long as what you try to do won't hurt anyone, they'll work like normal. Otherwise, they won't."

"Jason and Selby can jump or run across the planet," Sasha said, gritting her teeth, "but if they punch someone, their powers fail? That makes no sense."

"Don't blame me. Blame God or whoever designed these things that made us mutants." Ryan threw up his hands. "I'm only repeating what I heard."

"Wait," Rhapsody said. "Are you sure they don't do anything else?"

"Well, yeah. You age a whole lot slower, and you're sterile."

Selby scratched his temple. "Umm. . .what does 'sterile' mean?"

"It means, while you're wearing it on your body, you can't have kids," I said.

He grinned a mile wide. "Oh, this couldn't get *any* better."

Selby was in heat, and I'd do almost anything for a hot meal and a bed, at this point. "We have to get off the grid," I said. "Can you meet us in Walsh, Ryan?"

Ryan leaned back against the alleyway wall. "Why *Walsh*? You have a horse and buggy hookup? What's out there?"

I gave him the coordinates to the Collective's underground fortress and repeated them until he memorized them.

"Secret fortress, right?" he asked. "See you there."

Ryan left us in the alley and disappeared in the crowd. I walked with Sasha to the back of the alley. With the sun still in the sky, I'd need to be invisible, although it would be dark when we landed. Rhapsody had to go with me.

"I don't like this one bit, Jason," she said, wringing her hands together. "I wish my power was different, or something. Selby creeps me out. He's extra grabby."

"Yeah," I crossed my arms. "He's too fast for me to hit."

"I'm sure you hate being with Rhapsody all the time."

I looked away. "We don't get a choice, do we?"

Sasha cradled my face. "When things slow down, we need to talk."

After a quick kiss, I rejoined Rhapsody, who was wearing her mask. "Ready?"

It wasn't fair – she was hiding from me. "Yeah."

I bent down to cradle her legs in my arms – the way I normally held her, but she hesitated. "What's the problem?" I asked her.

"Can you hold me differently from now on?"

Are we going to do this now? "Yeah, if you want me to drop you. It worked fine the way we were doing it."

She flapped her arms at her sides. "Jason, it's just. . ."

"We don't have time," I said. "And I need you."

My answer broke her defenses. I pulled down my mask and we leaped away.

We landed at the cornfield first. The shine of the full moon gave us a little light to work with. Rhapsody and I stood there, starving, exhausted. I had no idea how they washed these bodysuits, but mine had sand and dirt on the outside and two days of sweat on the inside. I was afraid to unzip it past my neck and suffocate on my own stench.

The entryway didn't open. Maybe they were waiting for us to call them. That would suck. Our phones were somewhere on the eastern coast of Mexico. Hopefully they'd see us on their monitor and get to us before King could pin down our exact location.

Hands on my knees, I bent over and unmasked. Sweat dripped from my forehead and temples down to my neck. Rhapsody turned her back to me, took off her mask, unzipped her suit and breathed a loud sigh of relief. At that distance, with no breeze, she couldn't smell me. I eased my arms from my bodysuit and breathed. The night air cooled my sweltering skin. The extra necklace I'd taken dropped onto the dirt. I patted the ground, found it, and secured it inside my bodysuit's chest pocket.

"Jason," Rhapsody softly said. She turned around to face me and brushed her hands through her moist hair. "I. . .what I told you before. . .I. . ."

We heard a faint *pop* coming in from the far south. Selby and Sasha. Blazing a trail of corn stalks en route, they slowed down about a football field away. By the time they reached us, Selby was running at a normal speed. He carried Sasha pretty much the way I did Rhapsody – except my hand didn't stray to her butt the way his did to Sasha's.

Sasha jumped out of his arms and patted herself like she was covered in roaches. She looked at me and held her hands out, as if she expected me to do something. When I didn't, she sucked her teeth and flipped her hands.

"What's the deal, *Captain?* We're here. Why aren't the old folks opening up?"

I rolled my eyes at Selby's comment. "Don't know, *Leslie.* Maybe I should knock."

Arching my back, I raised my fists above my head and pounded the earth. In addition to creating two fist-sized holes in the earth, the strike sent a tremor through the immediate area. Soon we heard the *whirr* and *whizz* of the compound's entryway.

I looked at Rhapsody, who faked surprise by gasping. Sasha reluctantly smiled. I held out my arm in a "welcome" gesture. The girls walked inside, followed by

Selby. "Showoff," he said to me. I grinned as I brought up the rear.

We filed into the elevator. I stepped forward to close the elevator's gate and Selby pressed the "B" button. "You stink, *Freak,*" he said, holding his nose.

"Unzip," I shot back. "You won't smell springtime fresh, either."

Sasha, lip trembling, reached for my left hand. I held it and she laid her head on my shoulder. On the other side of me, Rhapsody cleared her throat and fixed her eyes on the see-through top of the elevator until we stopped in the basement.

When we entered the control room, Hughes was waiting for us with Courtney, who had returned and sat on her desk in a leather chair. At the sight of us, she lowered her head. She wore a bodysuit like ours and looked every bit as tired as we felt. Easing off of her desk, she walked tenderly in the direction of the bunks.

We'd screwed up. Majorly.

Hughes pointed his fingers toward Rhapsody and Sasha. "Go," he said with a heavy sigh. The girls trailed Courtney to the living quarters.

Hughes walked over to us. He wore black cargo pants, a matching knit shirt, army boots, and a utility jacket. Was he preparing to fight someone? "What in the world happened?" he asked us.

"We went after the white source," Selby said, "and. . ."

Hughes slowly shook his head. "No, no, no. See. I wasn't asking you because I didn't know the answer, Michael. I just wanted to hear your sorry explanation."

Selby set his shoulders square and approached Hughes, who was several inches taller than he was. "Who do you think you're talking to like that?"

"You," Hughes said, pointing his chin down. "You played a hand. You blew it. Man up and take responsibility for the mess you made. No one has time to coddle you."

His answer seemed to shut Selby down. I forced my lips to stop curling into a smile. Hughes must have seen it, or sensed it. "What are you so happy about, *Captain?*"

"Nothing," I said.

"You lost the goshenite. Did you even *think* about the scarlet emerald?"

The answer was obvious.

Hughes stiffened his posture. "Courtney went into the field and retrieved it."

"So, it all worked out?" I asked with genuine curiosity.

"You're missing the point, Jason."

"What *is* the point, *Brad?*" Selby shouted.

He crossed his arms over his chest. "You *have* to stop him. Otherwise, your home and anyone you ever even thought about will die, early and miserably. You want to know about King? That's what he does. He kills for whatever reason he sees fit."

The thought of my loved ones dying – even Ray and Julia – made me think. How long would it take for me to rebuild my life if *everyone* died? Susan had helped me piece myself back together after my mom passed. She wouldn't help me if we failed. She'd be at the bottom of the ocean with her husband, my family, and the rest of North America.

The texture of my new necklace was rough against my skin, so I pulled it out on top of my shirt. "That's better," I said.

Hughes' eyes widened. "Where did you get *that?* Do all of you have one?"

"I stole six of them," I responded. "King's got, like, twenty kids working for him. They all wear them. . .wore them."

"And you know what they do?"

Selby waved his hands. "Yeah, yeah, longer life, passive powers, no kids."

The fact we had done at least one thing right cracked through Hughes' tough guy act. "There's a corridor branching off of the bathroom," he said, smiling. "Hang your suits in there. Leftovers in the kitchen. Camuto was on the stove tonight."

"You should probably set an extra place," I said. "We invited a. . .*friend.*"

Just like that Hughes switched back to his rotten normal self. "You 'invited a friend'? As in gave the coordinates to this place to someone I didn't vet first?"

"Relax," Selby said, holding his hand out. "It's *Ryan Cain.* He's not that smart."

True, I hated him for obvious reasons, but I thought it through now. Had Ryan's girlfriend played him, or *had they played us?* Were they and King in it together? Was he going to tell King where we were and launch an attack on us for the provenance crystals? Ryan might not be that smart, but King was. After all, he'd been living for a long time.

Hughes cursed and pounded a fist on his desk. "You were in Orizaba, right? Fourteen kids, plus King. . ."

While he was thinking out loud, we stopped him. "No," I said, "*twenty* kids."

"When you stole the gold ice from them, did they shrivel up like Boris Karloff?"

Selby and I looked at each other. "Who?" we asked at the same time.

Hughes puffed out a long breath. "Did they get dark and brittle looking?"

I shrugged. "Yeah, I guess. Kind of."

"Then they're dead," he said without flinching. "And we have a little more than half a day before King gets here."

CHAPTER TWENTY

Showdown with Ryan Cain

I killed six people.

Ten hours from now, give or take – that's all Hughes figured King would need to mobilize an attack unit and move it from Mexico to Walsh.

"Of course, he could be wrong," Camuto said, "but I don't bet against him."

The four of us trickled into the dining room after our showers. Sasha and Rhapsody were already there, sitting across the table from one another. I sat in Hughes' spot, which put Sasha to my left and Rhapsody at my right. Tired of his "accidental" touches, Sasha made Selby sit next to Rhapsody.

We ate in silence. Our plastic forks scraping against the paper plates, our sipping from soda cans, and our chewing were the only sounds, except for an occasional belch by Selby. It was then I started thinking about how I could have been stupid enough to lead our enemies here. I did everything short of mapping it out on a GPS and jumping King to Walsh myself. Though I expected one of them, anyone, to blame me for it, no one did. Why not?

Courtney put us on a strict midnight curfew, which gave us a half hour to do whatever after we finished eating. On our beds lay new Geiger counter watches, upgraded cell phones, a sleeping pill and a bottle of water. Mine had six pills – one for sleeping and five Adderall for my ADHD. I glanced back at Sasha's bunk and she smiled while tying her hair back. Rhapsody was brushing her teeth in the bathroom. Selby was already a snoring lump under his green blanket.

I wandered to the source crystal room and found Courtney there. Wearing a long-sleeved white t-shirt and blue striped pajama bottoms, she sat cross-legged on the floor against the wall. When she heard the door's hinges, she waved me inside and patted the ground next to her. "Hi Jason," she said with a hoarse voice. "Join me?"

The glass shards from where I'd broken the window had been swept away. The alternate throbbing glow of the pink, red, and green crystals was like a light show. The colors on the walls changed from a dark pink to a weird shade of brown. I settled down next to Courtney. There, in the light, I noticed creases in her cheeks and wrinkles at the corners of her eyes. Has she gotten older? I thought the crystals stopped that.

"Not bad for an old lady, huh?" she asked me, focusing straight ahead.

"You read my mind?"

"No, you were staring. Much better than Michael, though. At least you're not always looking at my breasts."

I rested my elbows on my knees. "So, I basically gave a murderer our address and I killed six people."

She nodded and sighed. "Yeah. I heard."

"Why isn't anybody pissed off about that?" I pounded a fist on the floor, denting it. "I'm not a killer!"

Courtney turned her head in my direction. "Because we knew it was going to come to this at some point. We've been moving from place to place for years. This is our last outpost. He was going to find us here anyway. It was just a matter of time."

My eyes widened. "If you knew so much, why didn't you try to stop it? Why aren't you moving again? What makes right now any different?"

"You do."

I'd been afraid she was going to say that. "What do I have to do with it?"

Courtney licked her lips. Clearing her throat, she said, "After the last big solar storm forty years ago, the remaining eight split up. Welker and Peters went with King. Me, Camuto and Hughes stuck together."

I did the math. "Who are the other two?"

"One goes by Vivienne Coker. The other is Belinda King. You know them both."

My mouth dropped open. "W-w-wait! Who is Belinda King? King's sister?"

When it looked like she might answer me, Courtney avoided the question altogether. "Belinda built Reject High and Hidden Potential, Jason," she said. "She and Vivienne have been working together since the split. We're going to them for help."

"What kind of help?"

Courtney unfolded her legs and straightened up. "We're about to find that out. None of us have talked in forty years, but they'll know what we're up against."

I glanced down at my wrist. It would be midnight in five more minutes. "Alright," I said. "Good night. I'm off to bed."

"Jason?'

I opened my eyes to the cornfield, except it was golden yellow. There was someone else, a woman. Her thick, wavy black hair reached down past her shoulders. Her white linen dress had spaghetti straps. A purple scarf hugged her shoulders. She knew I was there. A quick turn of the head revealed her radiant smile, which I loved.

It was warm, a thick kind of summer heat, but I didn't mind. All I thought about was the woman. I called out her name. She turned around and waved, like we had not seen each other in a long time and I was a good friend. Her slender, rounded nose and the way her lips were formed – she reminded me a lot of Sasha. She was *perfect*.

My mother stood still and waited for me. *She's waiting for me. She wants me.*

"Mom," I called out to her, "I've missed you so much."

Her voice was sweet like pancake syrup. "Jason," she said, "I've missed you."

I ran over, almost close enough to touch her.

Bubbling over with emotion, she covered her mouth. "Jason!" she shrieked in a whisper. Her voice was different, distorted, almost panicked.

"Jason! Wake up. Something's happening."

Someone shook my body. Keeping my eyes closed, I wished they would go away and my dream to continue. All I saw in my mind's eye now was the back of my eyelids.

"Whaaat?" I slurred, wiping the drool from my face against the pillowcase. I wasn't even sure who was talking to me. "Time is it?"

It was Rhapsody. *Where are Sasha and Selby?*

"King. He's here. Get up."*How is that even possible?* I swung my legs over the side of the bed and jumped down to the floor. Rhapsody ran through the wall. While she was gone I snatched the extra gold ice necklace I'd stolen and put it underneath my sheets.

She returned a minute later, out of breath but carrying clean bodysuits. "Here," she said. "We've got to get out of here."

We dressed and pocketed our new cell phones. "Source room," I said through my mask.

"Source room," she said, pulling her mask on as well.

Rhapsody grabbed my hand and we passed through the corridors of the compound until we reached the storage area. Camuto had told us to keep our distance from the pink source. Now we were standing a foot away from it.

I heaved the morganite onto my left shoulder. Shaped like a giant football, it was difficult to get a hold of. "I'm going," I said, looking at the ceiling.

"Then, I'm coming," she said, moving close to me. "Go!"

We ghosted through the compound and streaked across the dark sky in an arc to the other side of Walsh, where Hidden Potential was located. There was an acre or so of trees beyond the main facilities. Once we had dropped the morganite there, we journeyed back to the room and moved the emerald next, leaving it beside the pink.

When we returned for the scarlet emerald, King's footmen crowded the room. Ryan, their leader snapped his fingers. "Julio, Luis."

Luis and Julio, identical twins, held us while another boy unzipped our bodysuits down to our waists and took our heliodor necklaces. He checked the inside pockets and patted us down, leaving us with our new cell phones. After all, we had no one to call now and they would explode soon, killing us anyway.

While he searched us my right leg suddenly gave out, and I fell to one knee.

"Jason!" Rhapsody called out. Luis blocked her from helping me.

Ryan grinned and held out his right hand. It was decorated with a goshenite ring, like King's. "No need to bow, Champion," he said. "But since you are. . ."

He kicked me across the left side of my face. I felt my cheek and temple swelling, and a stream of blood dribbling down my ear. "Not even. . .yet," I said, grimacing.

He approached the red source in the wall. Pulling a prism free for himself, he taunted me, "Don't you hate Julia? You *should* be thanking me for almost killing her. Nobody replaces your real parents, anyway."

The twins gave Ryan a look, like he had broken some sort of rule by taking a prism. Was he supposed to do that?

He shrugged them off. Pointing his thumb over his shoulder, he said, "Load up the scarlet emerald. Keep Selby and Sasha away from them."

They followed his orders. We were left with Ryan and two Caucasian boys.

Pushing off with my good leg, I got to my feet. "I'll beat your. . . on one leg."

Ryan approached me and grabbed my chin. "You can't even breathe."

"No," I said, spitting in his face. I could still do that.

He wiped his face with his forearm and punched me in the stomach.

Rhapsody sprang forward and shoved Ryan to the floor, daring him to hit her back. "Bring it," she said, motioning with her hands for him to get up. "I can take you."

Instead, he pulled a pistol from the holster on his leg and fired three times.

The first shot grazed me in the left arm. The second found a home under my shoulder blade. The last one landed right near my heart.

The world around me spun. I fell backward onto the floor, my arms spread out. My heart beat hard and loud. Bullets? Goshenite? I couldn't tell. I didn't care. It hurt.

Rhapsody called out my name. She was rushed away, by the twins, I guess.

Ryan bent down over me and patted my face with his hand. I was dying. For a moment he looked as if he regretted pulling the trigger.

"Following orders," he said with sincerity. "If it was up to me, I wouldn't have killed you this fast. But King's going to become a *god* soon. You're in the way."

His statement was the last thing I remembered hearing for a while.

CHAPTER TWENTY-ONE

collecting on a debt

Groaning with every move, I rolled to my side and used my hands to prop myself up. The wounds were too deep to tell what Ryan had used on me, goshenite or bullets.

Blood soaked my t-shirt and oozed down my body. At this rate I didn't have much time left. I needed to get to my bunk. I'd hidden my last gold ice prism there.

One. . .two. . .three. I stepped my hands back and slid my body a foot across the floor. I looked up to keep my focus off of all the blood. I hate seeing blood.

I thought of what Rhapsody had said about dying with no regrets. There were things I wished I had done. Sasha deserved to know the truth. Something was missing between us.

I had never told Rhapsody she was pretty. That *something missing* between Sasha and me? Rhapsody had buckets of it. *But who breaks up with the prettiest girl in school?*

One. . .two. . .three! I moved back another foot or so and coughed up blood. I closed my eyes, turned my head, and spat it onto the floor.

I didn't hate Ray, but he had pissed me off all the years he paid no attention to me. There was always work or some problem he had to fix with a client. Then it was about Julia. Then, *nothing*. After my ADHD and the rage blackout incident with the knife, he didn't want me anymore. I was one issue he just couldn't repair.

One. . .two. . .three! Almost there. My heart felt like it might give out any second.

Would anyone find me down here? This place, I was sure, did officially exist. At least this time I wouldn't be dying under ten feet of dirt. I used to want to be buried next to my mom. If I didn't get out of here, I'd see her soon, and it wouldn't be an issue.

I believed in God almost as much as I questioned Him. *Why did He make me different? Will I get to Heaven to be with her?* Maybe I wouldn't. *Does it even exist? If it does, and He's there, I plan to ask Him. The answer should be pretty good, I think.*

Finally at the door, I reached up and unlatched it. Using my upper body weight as a doorstop, I swung my left leg out into the hallway.

One. . .two. . .three!

I bent my right knee slightly and set it out next to my other leg.

Great, now I'm facing the wrong way.

Lying across the floor was a shriveled brown paper bag of a person sitting on her knees. Camuto? Courtney? Whoever she was, her clothes hung off of her. Her hair, thin and brittle, was completely white. Filmy brown eyes sank into her eye sockets. She crawled over to me, like an infant, and grabbed my left heel.

She gathered herself to stand. How, I didn't know. With freakish strength she started dragging me away by my foot. We passed through two doorways into the control room, where she stopped moving. There were two other people there. The larger one face down on the floor had to be Hughes, making the other one propped against a desk Camuto or Courtney. Neither of them spoke.

"My. . .bunk. . ." The blood loss made me woozy.

Hughes low-crawled over and climbed on top of me. He couldn't have weighed more than eighty pounds, but having him lie on me made it even harder to breathe.

"*Hoooooold. . .*" he croaked over my mouth. "*Onnnnnnn. . .*"

In a flash of yellow light we were inside of the bunk area, right next to my bed. *He teleported us!* Hughes rolled over onto the tiled floor and closed his eyes. A trail of golden mist wafted through the air.

Eyeing the top bunk, I grabbed the bed's support pole and willed myself to one foot. While standing I jabbed my hand underneath the covers until I sensed an area warm to the touch.

With the gold prism in my palm, I felt renewed. My body spit out the bullets Ryan had shot into it and sent them rattling across the floor. They were made of goshenite, after all.

I stepped into the bathroom and tore off my white shirt, stained completely red everywhere but the sleeves. There was no sign that I had been shot, not even a scar! *If someone takes off my prism, will the wounds return?* I didn't want to find out.

Gotta get rid of the blood.

I returned to the bunks. Hughes was gone. He must have teleported out to the control room. I'd meet him and the others there.

I entered the shower. Still with my suit on, I scrubbed at my exposed skin and let the water rinse away the rest. I realized something. I had bled so much that the water at my feet had turned pink. A retch rose in my throat. I almost threw up inside of the walled-in stall.

Feeling myself choking up, I let my emotions go and I cried over it all. My tears mixed with the water streams and dashed down my face in waves. Susan said crying was a healthy, normal thing to do. It felt terribly weak and exhilarating to me, all at the same time. I'd been on the edge of losing absolutely everything and I would, if I didn't do something. I dried my face with my towel and blinked the last tears away.

Thinking about the Collective, I hurried. Shutting the water valve off I shook off the remaining moisture. The suit did not absorb water but repelled it. Now I was ready to rescue my friends, take care of these provenance crystals, and break Ryan's face again.   When I returned to the control room, I found one of the women tending to Hughes and the other woman. Both were laid out on beds with IV bags.

"Courtney?" I asked, looking for a sign of recognition in her face.

She grumbled long and low and concentrated on what she was doing. Then I noticed she was wearing a shirt slightly different than Courtney's.

"Amauri?"

She nodded her head forward, like the weight of the world balanced on her skull. "You'll get over. . .seeing blood," Camuto said. Her voice crackled and hissed as she spoke. "Takes time."

It was good advice. "King has the white and red. I dropped the pink and green at Hidden Potential."

"Not much time," she growled.

I glanced over at the monitor hanging from the ceiling. Red, green, white, and pink dots were clustered in a spot no more than two inches from our location. Still missing were the gold and blue. Swiping my hand over the glass, like I'd seen King do, I switched the display. A blob of gold people were practically on top of the fortress. One of them was a reddish tone – that must be Ryan. My nostrils flared at the sight of him.

"Where do I find the missing ones?"

"Dome." Camuto coughed, her voice faltering. She pointed to her desk.

I rushed over and looked through the drawers for anything important. The one thing I found looked like a large remote control. I pressed its largest button.

The metal floor rumbled and parted in the middle. Below it was a rounded structure the size of a large bedroom. The surface was stone on the outside. No telling what was on the inside, but it had to contain nuclear-level radiation. She wanted me to drop the crystals into that thing. I could do that after I found my friends.

Pushing the button again closed the floor. I figured the button underneath it retracted the roof, or gave me an exit to get this thing out.

Camuto wavered and almost fell. I ran to her, lifted her frail body in my arms and laid her onto a spare bed. Next to it were an IV stand, tubes, and a needle. I always left the room every time the nurse stuck my mom in the hand. *How do you do this?*

". . .return," Camuto said, licking her cracked lips. "Save. . .*them.*"

I rubbed my forehead. "And you, too."

"I'm one hundred. . .seventy," she managed. "Don't. . .wanna live. . ."

Leaving them in this condition was difficult, but I couldn't save them by giving up my crystal. Not if I was the only one left to stop King. I rounded the bed and stopped at Hughes. "Solomon," I said close to his ear. "You saved my life. I'll be back for you."

His eyes opened and focused on me. He blinked twice, as if to say, "Alright."

Last, I went to Courtney. She looked as bad as Camuto, wrinkled and dark brown. Her bushy blonde hair was a dusty mop of thin gray strands now. The rest of her body was skeleton-bony and fragile-looking. "Don't worry," I said as she looked at me. "I'm not staring at your boobs."

Courtney laughed into a hacking fit. "Luck. . ." she said between coughs.

Examining the display, I realized King and his people were probably within earshot of the entryway to the fortress. If I opened it, they would figure out I was alive. "Why aren't they moving?" I wondered out loud. Courtney, Camuto and Hughes all slept peacefully. They were dying of bone cancer and needed heliodor. Where could I find help – someone smarter than I was and on the outside with powers?

I palmed my phone and stared at the wide-face display. With no other choice, I internet-searched Mr. Peters and found his home number. Taking a deep breath, I punched in his number and hit the green call button. It rang once.

"Hello?" said a woman, a *really young sounding* woman. She giggled. "Hello?"

"Is Jeff Peters there?" I asked.

Someone else snatched the phone. "Hello?" asked a different, just as young sounding woman. "Hello?"

"Jeff Peters," I said, gritting my teeth. "Is he there or not?"

"You sound cute," she said. "What's your name? Wanna come over?"

I rolled my eyes. The phone muffled for a few seconds before Peters finally picked up the receiver. "It's 6:15 in the morning. Who is this?" he demanded.

"Jason Ray Champion, Jr. You're going to help me. I saved your life."

"Get out!" he shouted to the girls in the background. "I need to be alone."

"Okay, okay," one of them said.

Peters waited until they closed the door behind them. "You must be in pretty bad shape if you need to collect a life debt from me."

The worst. I rubbed my eyes. "I'm stuck underground with your friends. King has four of the provenance crystals, and they're all going to explode soon. I need help."

"Let it go. Celebrate your young life while you can, Jason. The world is going to *burn*. What makes you believe that you can stop King and put it out?"

A month ago Principal Welker had asked me the same question and I had never answered him. What was my "will to power?" I thought about it for a few seconds.

"I'm *fifteen*," I said back to him. "Are you going to help me or not?"

Peters laughed. "I'm getting dressed. Tell me everything."

CHAPTER TWENTY-TWO

So screwed over

I told Peters all the details I thought he should know, about the crystals, my kidnapped friends, and the state of the Collective. Then he hung up on me.

From his house in the Heights to here couldn't be longer than a half-hour trip. I could wait that out. What if it was a trap, like the one Ryan pulled? I didn't want to think about it.

After a while watching twenty gold blips on the screen got tiresome. Being in the room with three two-hundred-year-old cancer patients was _really_ depressing.

My stomach rumbled, so I excused myself to the kitchen. I fumbled around the coffee maker long enough to figure out where to put what and made myself some.

A box of breakfast bars, two cups of coffee and a half box of Pop Tarts later my stomach was full. King and his people hadn't moved. Peters wouldn't answer his cell phone. An hour-and-a-half had passed and I was trapped in the compound.

"Wait." I said out loud to myself. "The TV!"

I made my way to the lounge and played with the buttons and switches. Finally one of them produced a buzz of electricity and the television turned on. Except it wasn't a television – it was the screen for their surveillance system. Three different points-of-view popped up beside the larger, main one. "Nothing but corn and weeds. Where are they?" I asked.

Eventually there was movement in the middle screen and the faint sound of a car engine. Still out-of-view, the ignition stalled and shut off. I heard a door opening then shutting and the sifting of moving corn.

"Diane!" yelled a hoarse male voice.

Was it Peters?

The middle camera showed the rising entryway to the fortress from behind. I rushed back through the control room and faced the elevator. As it rumbled and descended, I prepared to fight, just in case whoever it was tried to kill me.

Instead, Peters was in a little better condition than he had been in the hospital. His skin had a deep tan and creases that were turning into wrinkles. The muscles in his arms had sagged. He groaned and slumped against the control panel.

Pulling back the gate, I put his arm around my shoulder and helped him walk to the control room.

Breathless, Peters relaxed once I put him on the last of the beds. He reached out his right hand. Of the emerald crystals I had given him, only *one* was left. Peters rolled it into his slender fingers and gave it to me.

When I touched it, the radiation from the green had a different "taste" than the gold. Without it, Peters' condition rapidly worsened, so I gave him my heliodor prism. The aging process reversed on him, but not completely. Now, he appeared to be a healthy sixty-year old man. He stared at the bodies of his dying old friends. *What must he be thinking about them right now?*

"A little better," he said, rolling his neck around until his bones cracked. He walked over to the display screen. "I disabled their monitoring system. Go to the surface and get the crystals back. Leftover radiation keeps us alive, but not for long."'

"Hold on. How did you disable the monitoring system?" I asked while securing the green crystal into my necklace setting.

He gave me a knowing look. "They were monitoring you. I *disabled* them."

My eyes widened with disbelief. *He killed kids my age.*

He sighed heavily. "This isn't the movies. You don't knock them unconscious and leave. They have gold ice. They'll survive, come back in bigger numbers. They'll *end you*. And they're not kids. They've been alive longer than you think."

"I don't *kill*, not even King," I said, not totally sure I meant it.

Peters smacked me on the shoulder. "Policemen kill criminals. Governments execute dissidents. Armies bring down violent regimes. You have that kind of authority now, whether you like it or not. Grow up and use it. Stop acting weak."

I shook my head. "What if I don't want it?"

Peters folded his arms over his stomach. "Whatever. I don't owe you anymore." He pointed his index finger toward the Collective. "People are going to die, no matter what – including them and your family, if you don't do anything."

Hughes and Courtney had risked a lot for me. Camuto probably had, too. "How do I get back in here?" I asked him. "Yell out 'Diane' like you did? Who's Diane, anyway?"

Peters released a small, notepad-sized keyboard from the side of the display and started tapping keys, like he was familiar with it. "That's *my* wife's name, my code, synced to *my* voice," he said, his eyes suddenly cold. "I'll program one for you. A name is fine. And don't ask me about her again."

"What about Rhapsody, and Sasha, and Selby? How can they get in here?"

"Not without you. That's their problem." He smirked. "If you want them to actually survive, you'd better get going. I'll take care of these three."

I rushed to the elevator and closed the mesh gate. While inside it, I tapped the unmarked button and saluted Peters. It was the closest thing to a "thank you" he was going to get out of me. Amazingly, he saluted me back, saying "Captain." After all this time, I guess I was finally getting used to it.

"Crap!" I shouted as daylight flooded the entryway. "Peters, what's my code?"

He didn't answer me and I didn't have enough time to go back downstairs. When the time came, I'd have to guess it. Hopefully it was something simple and not a trick.

Once I was outside and the opening to the compound shut, I heard the rhythmic sound of helicopter blades. *Are there three sets? Four?* I couldn't tell. Blood rushed to my head and throbbed in my ears. My heart raced. They were approaching fast.

"Alright, Jason," I said, wiggling my gloved fingers. "Run or fight? Run? Or *fight?*" I could jump away faster than they could zap my powers with white ice. My friends would still be in captivity if I left. Two provenance crystals were on the loose and there were the two I had ditched at Hidden Potential. Running wasn't the answer.

"Okay then," I said, cracking my knuckles. "Now, what's next?"

I tugged my mask down over my face and inhaled the air circulating through the mouthpiece. From twelve o' clock came three military helicopters flying in an "L" formation. The one at the longer part of the pattern had two propellers and was the largest.

Using my left hand to further shield my eyes from the sun, I gazed in the distance and cursed. *How did those things get across the border without being stopped?*

I had to think fast. Other than my body, I didn't have a weapon. *Peters.* I dialed the compound from my phone. "Where's your car?" I asked Peters when he picked up.

"Nine o'clock, twenty yards out. It's old, so hotwire it. The clutch sticks a bit and. . . ." he said, before catching himself. *"Wait.* You can fly. Why do you need to drive?"

Why do people keep saying I can fly? "Driving it's not what I had in mind."

I took a short jump over to his Jupiter, lifted the car by the side of the chassis, and used it as a two-ton shield. With its width blocking my entire body, I walked toward the *chop chop chop* sounds.

Suddenly the pilots fired at me. The rounds went *rat-tat-tat-tat-tat* into the plastic shell of Peters' car, but they did not penetrate through it. For the second time in less than a day, I hoped to God it wasn't goshenite.

The barrage continued and cut through the chassis, shattering the windshield and passenger side windows. The blasts started hitting metal parts and ricocheting off of them. I stepped over pieces of the Jupiter as they dropped off. This wasn't working.

Letting the car down a foot or so, I peeked over its side. The helicopters were in plain sight, close enough for me to take them out. The two in the front were a regular size, but the one to their left was *huge – what is in there?*

Switching my grip to each side of the chassis, I yelled and flung Peters' car at the first helicopter. Its hood smashed right into the cabin. The middle and rear of the body flipped over into the rotors.

"Yeah!" I pumped my fist as the helicopter exploded in a burst of orange flame. Heliodor would protect them, so I didn't have to worry about killing anyone, after all. Some debris caught the other small helicopter and sent it into a wicked tailspin. It crashed to my left in a cloud of fire, tossed corn, and black smoke.

The only one left was the two-rotor helicopter. It lined up in front of me. Before it could open fire, I crouched down and leaped for it. When I came close enough to see Sasha, Rhapsody, and Selby tied up inside of the cabin, the helicopter vanished in a wisp of gold mist. I soared far beyond it and landed miles away in a wheat field.

"Great," I said, thrusting my hands out. "A disappearing helicopter."

I turned around and jumped back to the two-helicopter wreckage. None of the passengers were conscious. Three or four were pinned under the burning wreckage. It smelled like burning skin and hair. I searched around for anything I thought might be useful. Written on a burning piece of paper wedged into a control panel was a set of coordinates. The right edge of it had burned off the last number.

Peters had a point. They would come after us. I stripped all of the occupants of their gold prisms. Without heliodor, they aged at a slower rate than Peters and the Collective had, settling around fifty years old or so.

I dropped all of the prisms at the base of the compound's hidden entryway and flashed Peters a "thumbs up" sign.

The others and Camuto would live to see another day, even if they didn't want it. I'd be back for the dome.

CHAPTER TWENTY-THREE

somebody is going to die

Having ADHD means that with things going on around me all of the time, focusing on one of them is a challenge.

That wasn't my problem here. *Nothing* was happening. I could barely see the explosion I'd caused. Soon ambulances and fire engines would scramble to the scene.

The emergency personnel might have a hard time figuring this one out. How had a group of over-tanned senior citizens crashed two helicopters in the middle of nowhere?

Oh well. It was their problem, not mine.

Someone was running at me from behind. I heard the cornstalks parting. With fists clenched, I swiveled my hips and threw my hardest punch. I missed and lost my balance, falling face first into the dirt. Good thing I still had my mask on.

"Stay on your knees," said a male voice with a Spanish accent. "They're coming."

When I got my bearings, the boy put his hand on my shoulder. I glanced at his face and did a double take. He looked *a lot* like the twin brothers Ryan had with him.

"*Esteban,*" he whispered, like he knew what I was thinking. "Not Luis or Julio."

"What's the difference?" I blurted it out, louder than I should have.

"Shh," he said with urgency. "Trust me. There's a *big* difference."

The level of my voice must have alerted them to our position. A flurry of gunshots rang out in our direction.

Esteban, with his hand still on my shoulder, teleported us to another section of the field. Goshenite rocks landed close to our feet. We still weren't safe.

Then he moved us to the grove of trees at the edge of the cornfield where I'd left the source crystals. Altogether, he must have popped us in and out across a few miles.

When we stopped moving I gasped and cursed, patting my body to make sure it was solid again. Trails of gold smoke drifted from the fibers of my bodysuit. I unmasked to let myself breathe.

Esteban's laugh was coarse and annoying. "You get used to it," he said. "Cool costume. I could use one of those."

We weren't alone. To my left was a curly-haired blonde my age. Next to her, a short, brunette girl grinned at me. She looked like the other girl's sister.

"They're on the attack. We have to get the others and mobilize," Esteban said, his voice shaking.

The others? "What's wrong?" I asked him. "You okay?"

He spat on the ground and pointed up in the sky. "They're starting. Look."

There were no clouds to shield the sun's strength, so I pulled my mask down. Even then, I couldn't look at it for long. What I saw was amazing!

A small, round mass of sunlight bulged out from the sun's right side. Like a balloon, it filled up to its capacity and burst, sending an explosion of vibrant yellow rays streaking across the sky. I didn't have to ask Esteban what he meant.

Bending over, I closed my eyes and rolled over onto the lush grass. The earth was spinning in my head, more than like the night Hughes and I had drunk scotch.

Before long all four of us were on the ground, moaning and clutching our stomachs. Thankfully, it lasted a short time. But when it stopped I felt increased power flowing through my system, like I had guzzled a dozen power drinks back to back.

Esteban examined his hands as if they were glowing. "You guys feel that?"

The blonde girl's head bobbed with enthusiasm. "Uh huh? Do you, sis?"

"Yeah," said the brunette. Her voice squeaked. "It tingles."

I didn't like where this was going. If solar flares made us stronger, wouldn't our enemies be affected, too?

"We have to stop them *here*," I said. "But they're invisible. The solar flares aren't helping, and without white isotopes we can't see them."

"White isotopes?" Esteban repeated. "You must mean *goshenite.*"

"Whatever." I waved my left hand. The glare from the glass face of my Geiger counter flashed in my eye. "You said I'll get used to it –the teleporting?"

"Yeah," he said. "It's a focus thing. I'm ADD, so even I get sick of it sometimes. The adrenaline helps, I think."

He's ADD, too? "Hmm." My eyebrows rose. "Here's what we're going to do. We're going to go into the field together. We'll take them out, one by one, until we get the one who's making them invisible. One of them has to know where King is."

Esteban clapped. "Dangerous and risky. I like it! Good deal! I'm in."

"We can cast a force field pretty wide," said the blonde. "When we see you, we'll throw it up. Won't keep out goshenite for long, though."

"I'll pop us out," Esteban said.

He didn't sound sure of himself. "You can teleport all of us?"

"Not far" was all he would say about it. "Stay close. I have to be able to see you at all times."

With that, he teleported us back to where he had found me. We stood, back to back, and rotated around, listening, watching. My watch clicked a few beats.

One of our enemies was close, but *how close?*

I swept my arm in the air, creating a semi-circle. I stopped when the clicks became stronger. They could hear it, too. Esteban elbowed me in the shoulder, right before one of them shot at us.

I caught three rounds of goshenite in the stomach before I pinned down his location.

"At your six o'clock!" I grunted.

Esteban popped us in the exact direction I'd told him. I lunged forward and tackled the boy to the ground. Grabbing his weapon, I placed my left foot on his chest and shot him a couple of times. He must have the invisibility power, because the rest of his crew appeared once he was down.

I sprayed shots at them. The goshenite hit the five other boys. Two of them were close to us.

Esteban went to each and stripped them of weapons and gold ice. He kept one of their guns and threw the rest of it into the air. They vanished in a burst of gold smoke.

"Didn't know you could do that," I said to him. Pulling goshenite rocks out of my skin was always painful, but with my bodysuit's protection, it didn't hurt as much.

He shrugged. "Me, neither."

"Where's King?" I asked the guy underneath my foot. I took his necklace. His skin darkened and wrinkled like a raisin. He couldn't answer me.

I moved on to one of the other boys and pointed my gun at him. "Where's King?"

"Castling," the boy said from his dry lips.

A city named "Castling?" I didn't know of any in the state. Maybe King was somewhere farther away than we thought.

"Dude," Esteban said from between clenched teeth. "Can you move?"

My leg muscles seized so I couldn't jump away. Then the paralysis spread to the rest of my limbs. My heart skipped one or two beats and I stopped breathing. The flare had expanded Ryan's power. He could control my organs now, too.

I heard his ridiculous laugh behind my back. "New powers are something else."

He'd even frozen our eyes open. It didn't hurt me, but I could tell Esteban was suffering. The last time Ryan mind-controlled me, it didn't last long if I tried to escape. I couldn't link together my thoughts, even though I'd taken Adderall this morning.

"I don't know how you survived," he said, walking around us. Ryan cocked his gun. "This time I'll watch you die."

"You're going to fail," I said. "Always do."

Ryan shot Esteban in the chest before he could think to teleport. "Not this time."

Esteban grunted in pain, but stood still. A small circle of blood appeared on his white baseball shirt and dribbled a line down to his waist.

Esteban crumpled to the ground and Ryan stepped over his body. He smiled back at me. "You're next," he said.

If I didn't do something, try something, Ryan would murder him.

Summoning everything inside me, I concentrated on rushing Ryan. My effort broke through his mental grip. He turned around too late to stop me.

I flew forward, my shoulder thrusting into his gut. We brushed through the fields at a ridiculous speed. I wanted to slow down or stop, but couldn't. I was in the hallway at North High School all over again, and he was making fun of my mother. Something inside of me broke and reining it in wasn't an option anymore.

Hughes was right. Killing him was on the table.

I finally planted my feet and slid to a stop in a grass field. Ryan tumbled for a quarter mile before landing face down. Jumping over to Ryan at once, I turned him over. Blood, dirt, and grass stains streaked across his face. His clothes were shredded. I patted around his collar and broke his red ice chain off his neck. I tossed it as high as I could throw it and threw mine next to a nearby tree. It would be a fair fight.

Gasping for breath because of my lung, the pain in my leg, and the bullet wounds, I balled up my fists and punched Ryan with everything I had. He tried blocking my punches, but I was too strong for him. Over and over I smashed my fists into his face until he fell unconscious. We still weren't even.

Hughes had said Ryan would come back with reinforcements and kill me. Now I believed him. He had to die here.

CHAPTER TWENTY-FOUR

the real fight starts

I limped over to the tree and retrieved my emerald. Its power revived me. My bad lung inflated and the ligaments in my knee mended better than new.

In the next few moments I'd kill Ryan Cain.

Before I got to him Esteban teleported in and interrupted me. "Stop," he grunted out. "The girls have the force field up. We gotta go."

"No," I said, bumping his shoulder as I passed him.

He popped in front of me again. "Murder him and you're no better than King."

My arm muscles quivered. "Move or *I'll move you.*"

Esteban stepped aside and held up his hands in surrender. "You got it."

I grabbed Ryan by the neck and lifted him off the ground. His head bobbed.

Raising my fist to deliver the death blow, I looked over at Esteban, expecting him to teleport my enemy away. He broke eye contact with me. I was on my own. When I let Ryan go he fell awkwardly to the ground. My confidence shrank a little. As much as I wanted to rid myself of him forever, I couldn't bring myself to do it.

"Whew." Esteban wiped his brow. "Thought you might actually kill him."

I swallowed hard and made a shooing motion with my hands. "Can you. . ."

He held his palm in Ryan's direction and made him disappear in gold smoke. "He won't do anything to you now, not where I put him. We need to head back."

In a moment we were inside Hidden Potential's borders. I recognized most of the buildings from the brochures I'd seen. King's helicopter had landed in the camp's main square next to the flagpole. Nobody was guarding it.

Inside it, tied down to the seats, sat Sasha and Rhapsody. Selby slumped between them. The source crystals King had stolen were gone.

I reached across Selby and yanked Sasha's and Rhapsody's binds at the same time. Both of them had the instinct to hug me, but Sasha nudged Rhapsody to the side and got to me first.

"Oh, God, Ryan said you were dead," Sasha said, kissing me on the cheek.

From behind Sasha's back, I watched Rhapsody. She didn't say anything, but her watering eyes did. She wiped her tears away.

While the girls gathered themselves Esteban checked Selby's limp wrist for a pulse. "Not good news over here,"

Turning my attention to Esteban, I asked him, "Got green crystal anywhere?"

"Emeralds?" he asked. "Ms. Coker doesn't keep any around, so we don't kill each other. We'll have to go to the pit for it."

I understood that. Giving aggressive superpowers to teenage criminals sounded like a bad idea.

Rhapsody scowled. "And 'the pit'? Doesn't sound like a place we need to go."

"I'm open to other ideas," Esteban said, folding his hands at his waist. "Got any?"

We looked at Sasha. "None over here," she said.

Seeing as I was the super-strong one, I drew the short straw. Tossing Selby over my shoulder, I said, "Well, it's not like we have all day."

In a blink Esteban transported us to the pit site, which was in a field behind the campground. Nine of King's people, dressed in all black, were gunning for the campers.

The sisters were at the forefront of the battle, straining to keep their golden force field strong enough to block the waves of goshenite and protect the pit.

Breathing heavily and sweating, Esteban dropped his shoulders and took several breaths through his mouth. "Need a minute," he said before teleporting away.

With nowhere to hide in an open plain, I had to protect the girls. I clutched both of them around the waist and leaped to the closest building. We set down at its back steps. I returned a minute later with Selby, whose breathing was shallow.

From here the fight looked like a daytime fireworks show. "Stay here."

"You can't leave us here!" Rhapsody shouted at me.

For once Sasha agreed with her. "Not happening, babe."

I ran my hands through my hair. "You need green ice to fight, and it's in the pit."

Rhapsody sighed and pouted. "Fine," she said, crossing her arms. "We'll stay."

I didn't believe her for a second, but there was no time for debating.

With my mask on, I returned to the battle. The force field withstood the charge, but not without help. Vivienne Coker was there, casting the force field with the sisters. When I landed at the edge of the force field, she allowed me in and quickly closed it behind me.

"Jason." She said my name like she was acknowledging my presence.

"I need to get into the pit," I shouted over the gunshots and yelling.

She nodded back in its direction. "Hurry. We need help."

I raced over to the pit and lifted the cover. It looked identical to the dome at the fortress. A warm blast of light and radiation greeted me. The Geiger counter on my wrist clicked a thousand times a second. Inside were the emerald, morganite, and heliodor sources.

They had the gold one the entire time!

I eased down inside of the hole, which was the size of a well. The morganite was on top, which worried me because of what Camuto said – it released the heart's deepest desire. I didn't know mine and didn't want to know. Reaching down, I freed a bunch of green and gold prisms and placed them in the bodysuit pocket over my heart. Never hurts to have extras.

When I started climbing out, I overheard loud yells and cries of pain.

"Jason," Vivienne said. A gasp of pain cut her voice off. "Get out!"

The shooting stopped. It was around noon, so I looked up in time to see the end of the solar flare. The hum of energy vibrated under my feet.

Leaning against the pit's lead inside, I took deep breaths to stop the nausea. Sweat poured down my face and wet the inside of my suit. It hurt and lasted way longer than last time had.

I pulled myself up to the surface and closed the lid to the pit. The after-effect of the flare was stronger within me. With the force field still down, I leaped for the spot where I'd left my friends. Selby was sprawled out on the steps. Sasha and Rhapsody were both gone. I'd known they wouldn't stay. Small explosions erupted nearby – discarded cell phones.

Selby stirred when I brought one of the prisms close enough. "Thanks," he said, standing to his feet a minute later. "What did I miss?"

I pointed to the battleground where activity had resumed. "King's going after the provenance crystals. We're going to stop him."

"Uh huh," he said, nodding.

"Good guys are with Vivienne Coker. Bad guys have white ice, so be careful." I handed him two prisms. "Give these to the girls if you find them first."

"Gotcha." Selby raced off.

For the life of me I couldn't figure out why Sasha and Rhapsody would go off somewhere without powers and *together?* That was even weirder. I needed to find King and take him down. If I did that all of this would be over. Where was he?

Instead of joining Vivienne and the others, I jumped for the enemy camp and dropped behind their flank. I surprised two of them, ripped off their gold prisms, and tossed them far behind me.

One of the boys turned toward me and held out his palm, like Esteban does.

Oh crap.

A gold blur of smoke later I stood alone in a cornfield. I paused for a moment so I wouldn't vomit. "Hate. . .teleporting," I muttered.

Reciting the compound's coordinates, I jumped for it. I could grab the Collective for reinforcements and head back to fight.

When I arrived I ran through the possibilities of my entry code.

"Anna" was the first name I said. It didn't work. Peters knew everything else about me. He didn't know my mother's name?

Alright. Let's try again. "Debra. . .Zachary. . .Deidra. . .Ray. . .Julia. . .Selby."

Nothing. None of them worked.

I flapped my hands in frustration. "Sasha. Not *Sasha?* You've got to be kidding me, Peters. I don't have time for this! How about Rhapsody?"

I was halfway joking, but the entryway whirred open. Ducking down, I ran in before it fully opened, hurried down the elevator and into the control room.

The place had been trashed. The display screen had been torn down and shattered. Sparks popped from its crossed electrical wires hanging from the ceiling. The overhead lighting flickered every few seconds.

I stepped carefully around the broken glass and approached the infirmary. Hughes, Camuto, and Courtney lay there, motionless.

I gave each of them a gold and green prism and waited.

"We need to talk," said a familiar, gruff voice from the darkness.

Grabbing one of the unused IV stands, I tossed it like a spear in the direction of the voice. I must have missed, because he kept talking.

"Stop acting like a Neanderthal and listen to me boy!" he shouted before opening fire.

I held up my arms to protect myself, but I didn't need to. Hughes had revived and teleported me across the room to my assailant. I grabbed him by the throat and lifted him. The shine on his bald head and the gold prism dangling from his neck disappointed me. It was Ron Welker, my old principal from Reject High.

I tossed Welker through the control room wall and followed him through the hole. "Talk," I said as he coughed up blood onto the floor. "Where is he?"

Welker looked at me with cold eyes. "Castling."

CHAPTER TWENTY-FIVE

we lose and win

I'll be the first to admit it. I'm a terrible student.

Not that I was ever any good at school. When I was supposed to be doing make-up work after Reject High exploded, Sasha and I were hooking up. She was smart enough to skip the books and still make As. I wasn't. If I had opened one up every once in a while, I might actually know what "Castling" meant in history.

Welker kicked me through the hole in the wall he'd made. I hit the floor and slid, eventually rolling over onto my side. I checked my bodysuit pocket. The prisms were still there, for now. While he gave me time, I hid one of them inside my clothes in one place I hoped he'd never look.

He grabbed me by the ankles and swung me toward the contact room wall. I landed back first and dented the metal. Prying myself from the indentation, I got to my feet.

"That's all you got?" I asked, making a "come here" sign with my hands.

Out of nowhere one of the hospital beds flew at me. I caught it, tore its metal frame in half, and dove for Welker.

Swinging each side like a baseball bat, I smashed them into his head, one at a time. Then I clapped them together at his ears, bent them around his head, and punched him in the mouth. It might not have hurt my former principal much, but it sure confused the crap out of him.

Without my weapons, I uncorked my strength and pounded his body with everything I had. One thing about Welker being strong, I could hit him as hard as I wanted. He wasn't going to die that way, and I didn't plan to stop.

We continued fighting, but I always kept the advantage. It was like a no holds barred wrestling match. When we weren't hitting each other with our fists and feet, we grabbed objects and pummeled each other with them.

My opponent got the worst of it. I was getting bored. He was wearing down and bleeding from several spots on his face. *I'm actually hurting him?*

Eventually he'd have to give in. I'd keep going until he did.

While pretending to be seriously injured, Welker suddenly recovered and tried impaling me with a jagged piece of hospital bed frame. I dodged it in time.

The shard of metal disappeared in a stream of gold smoke.

"You don't need that right now, Ron," Hughes said.

I backed away to see the newly revived, three-member Collective.

Courtney sidled over to us. "This is the end, Ron," she said to him.

Welker staggered to his feet. He wiped the blood from his lips on the back of his hand. "Didn't you say the same thing *forty years ago*, Eris? No? Maybe it was in '89 or 2003? Perhaps 2006? Gosh, I can't remember. It's been over *so many times*."

Camuto came out from behind Courtney. "I said it after we contained them the first time. We *all* should have died then, and not. . ."

". . .but we *didn't*," he interrupted. "We're here. And now David will become immortal, and I'll sit at his right hand for two hundred years."

Hughes shook his head. "He stole your heliodor from your precious chess set. Otherwise, you wouldn't be here. Think, Ron. We'll all die if you're wrong."

He was hiding his heliodor in his chess set? That's why he made me play chess with him – he thought I had stolen the missing pieces.

"No theory becomes truth without a test!" Welker yelled. "Isn't that what Jeff used to quote us? You're an old slave, Solomon. No one expects you to understand."

Hughes seethed. "There's only one God, and He's not some Fidel Castro-looking knockoff with a little man complex."

"Why are we even talking about this?" I asked them. "Let me finish him off. I was winning."

Welker shook his head. "No, you weren't."

"You're the one bleeding," I said.

He flashed a red smile. "Regardless, you don't have the goshenite or scarlet emerald. But thanks to you we know the locations of the heliodor, emerald, and morganite."

Although I preferred to fight him, he had a valid point. I was stronger than he was, but he was *way* smarter than I was. Esteban and I had led him straight to them.

"The fighting stops for now and we negotiate," said Welker. "Peacefully."

Courtney paced back and forth. "What's it going to take? Does he allow you to answer, or do you wait until he pulls your strings?"

Welker put his finger at the corner of his lips. "Not quite. It's simple. He gets into the pit before the crystals blow. Unless one of you wants to volunteer, instead?"

Hughes looked at his partners for confirmation. "It's his funeral, right?" he said.

"*And* a piece of aquamarine," he added. "I almost forgot."

A blue prism? They didn't know where it was located. It was a big problem, considering it would trigger a thermonuclear explosion in less than a day. *Unless. . .*

"No way," I said. "Not gonna happen, Ron."

All of them, Courtney, Camuto, and Hughes stared at me.

I stuck my chest out. "Your ears don't work after two hundred years, either? Or did I stutter? Keep the scarlet, emerald and goshenite. Kill me, them, all my friends and family. Blow up half the freaking planet. But you're going with it."

Welker's skin paled. "You found the aquamarine?"

"But you'll never find it," I said, bluffing him. "Especially if *one* of my friends dies. Without it, King will be a pile of ash like the rest of us."

I watched my opponent for his reaction. His eyes narrowed, like he was concentrating on something. *Was he trying to read my mind again? Good luck with that.*

Usually I hated teleporting, but it was the fastest way back to the battle. "Hughes, can you send me back?"

His expression said he hoped I knew what I was doing.

Fallen bodies lay all over the singed grass. Most of them belonged to injured Hidden Potential campers. White stones the size of my thumb stuck out from their bodies in various places – necks, chests or arms. They were bleeding profusely and twitching with seizures.

They needed help almost as much as the group still standing.

Selby, Rhapsody, Sasha, Vivienne, the force field sisters and Esteban were surrounded by six gunners near the pit.

My friends were exhausted from fighting. It showed in their weary, slumped shoulders, bloody noses and drooping mouths. Fatigue kept Esteban and Selby from escaping. Rhapsody couldn't go invisible or ghost and Sasha wouldn't be able to clone.

How could I take out six people at once? Shooting the other guys with Esteban had been luck. These would be a little harder to hit, and if I missed, I'd be captured, too.

Suddenly a wave of nausea hit me. My vision blurred. I swooned and collapsed onto the grass. Rolling over to face up, I witnessed the latest round of solar flares. This time, two balloons of solar energy ruptured.

These things were getting much worse, faster than the forecasts had predicted. The episode lasted more than a few minutes. Again I recovered faster than anyone else.

I had an idea.

I blasted off into the sky above my friends, going higher than I had jumped before. Without my mask on I couldn't hear. My altitude peaked somewhere in the clouds.

I streaked towards the ground, feet first. When I got close enough I heard gunshots. None of them could lay a bead on me. I counted on that.

When my feet hit the ground between my friends and our enemies, they created a ripple effect. Sheets of earth swelled out from my landing point and swept everyone away in a massive wave of dirt. The boys and their guns flew off into the air.

The same thing happened to Sasha, Rhapsody and the others, except Vivienne wrapped them in a golden force field to lessen the impact.

When the tremors stopped I climbed out of the crater I'd created and met them on the other side of the damage. Esteban shook my hand. "Coolest thing I've ever seen."

"Yeah, whatever. Let's finish this," Selby said, disappearing in a *whoosh.*

We followed him around the hole over to the other side. By the time we got there, Selby had confiscated their gold ice. He handed everything to Esteban, who sent them away. I unhooked the ammunition clips and crushed the guns under my feet.

"So that's it?" Esteban said, dusting off his hands. "We won, right, Ms. Coker?"

Vivienne's face darkened. "Solar storm is tomorrow. He'll try again."

"We'll be ready, though, won't we?" he asked her.

I roamed around the scattered bodies and found Luis or Julio. Grabbing him underneath his armpits, I carried him over to where Vivienne and the others were standing. "Hi, everyone," I said, shaking him. "My name is. . ."

"Julio," Esteban said, identifying his brother.

Julio glowered at Esteban. "Traidor," he said in Spanish.

Even I understood what he was saying when it was that simple. "Julio is going to tell us where the scarlet emerald and goshenite are."

My Spanish was rusty, but I'm sure he didn't tell me where to find them. Confused, I turned to Esteban and Rhapsody to translate.

"What he told you to do to yourself isn't physically possible." Esteban tried not to laugh.

Rhapsody stepped forward. "Wise guy on deck! I've got this."

As I held Julio up Rhapsody ghosted her right arm completely through his body and held it there. She said something to him in Spanish before pulling her arm away.

Julio's entire body trembled. "A-alright, alright, I'll tell you."

CHAPTER TWENTY-SIX

a town called Traveller

With Rhapsody clinging to my back, I left for the location Julio had given us.

The directions were to Traveller – a town Walsh-like in size. Of course it had to be a trap, but Julio and Luis were along for the ride. Esteban made sure of that. Vivienne and the sisters stayed behind to guard the captives and tend to the injured. Taking them to the hospital would draw too much attention. The authorities couldn't handle this level of conflict, anyway.

With Esteban teleporting himself and his brothers, Sasha rode shotgun with Selby. This time, when he dropped her off, she didn't freak out as much. Her body language toward him was different. She didn't protest the touching as much.

Rhapsody noticed the change, too. I could tell by the mild surprise on her face as Selby's hands lingered on the small of Sasha's back. Sasha tapped his arm and giggled.

Unable to take it any longer, I pulled her aside by her elbow. "What was *that?*" I asked.

"What?" She pretended to have no clue what I was talking about.

"You and him!" I gestured with my hands. "Touching your back and what not?"

"Oh," she waved her hand. "Nothing. It's fine. A little harmless attention, that's all. Don't worry about it."

It wasn't "fine" but I didn't have time to go back and forth with her.

"There," Julio said, pointing. "They're in the backyard."

I looked around. Two-stories, with an open porch in the front, the whitewashed home looked old enough to have been around since the 1800s. Even in plenty of daylight the eerie, blackened windows made my skin crawl. I pictured someone watching us, an old, insane woman with rotten teeth and a terrible cackling laugh.

First Welker, now him. "What's with these guys and creepy looking houses in the middle of nowhere?"

The rusted wrought iron gate creaked as I pushed it open. We filed through one by one. Once we were inside I led the charge with Rhapsody at my side. The brothers stayed behind us. Sasha and Selby brought up the rear.

I peeked back once or twice at them. The two of them had gotten *way* too chummy. Who was I to talk, though? I'd made out with my best friend.

We picked our way through the weeds and circled the building. "Hard to believe someone actually lived here," I said.

"A lot of people lived here, once," Esteban said from the back. "It's an *asylum.*"

We stopped dead in our tracks. I had the urge to scratch my skin.

"Say what?" Rhapsody shuddered.

"It's true." Luis nodded. "It was a boarding house for the mentally ill."

Sasha hugged her arms around her body and leaned into Selby.

"That's it." I broke from the front and pushed Esteban and his brothers aside. Shoving Selby away from Sasha, I then took her by the hand. "What's going on with you? Trying to make me jealous is kind of childish."

She shook her hand. "Not even. Let me go!"

"Do it, *Freak.*" Selby cracked his knuckles and glared at me.

I gritted my teeth and released her. We had a planet to save, anyway.

When we reached the backyard, the sight of tombstones stopped everyone but Luis and Julio. Obviously, finding a graveyard behind an insane asylum wasn't weird to them. Or they had been here before.

A freshly shoveled mound of dirt was off to the edge of the rickety white wooden fence. My wristwatch Geiger counter went nuts. So did Sasha's, Rhapsody's, and Selby's.

"Okay." I ignored the rising fear in my stomach. "Dig up mutant crystals. In a cemetery. Behind a crazy house." No one spoke and nothing around us made a sound. "No problem."

With no tool to dig with, I'd have to use my hands. Thankfully, I had gloves. "Join me, Leslie!"

Esteban watched his defenseless brothers stand by while Selby and I went to work. With his speed, he cleared his part cleared in no time. I might as well have been standing to the side. Pulsating goshenite and scarlet emerald prisms peeked from out of the earth. They must have fallen off of the provenance crystal.

Jackpot! I reached down into the earth and touched something hard. With thick gloves on it was difficult to tell what it was, so I grabbed onto it tighter.

The inside of my stomach shifted when I grasped a handle.

I shifted my attention to the goshenite and scarlet emerald. "Need a second," I said, gesturing toward the hole. My hands were shaking. "Casket."

Rhapsody reached her arm around my shoulders and encouraged me to sit. "Breathe," she said in a gentle voice. "It's not your mom."

Sometimes I got this way in cemeteries. As much as I visited my mom's gravesite after finding out where it was, I'd get sick about every third time I went. Susan and I were supposed to discuss it at our latest session. But I'd hulked out and chucked her door into the ocean, so that was the end of that.

Rhapsody leaned me against a chipped granite headstone and fanned her hands at my face. Then she stopped to fan herself. Pulse racing, I suddenly felt weak.

Not again. More solar flares.

I glanced over at Esteban, who vomited in the bushes. Julio and Luis tossed their cell phones, hopped the fence and ran away. We were powerless to stop them.

Sasha clutched her stomach and Selby's face reddened.

I crawled onto the ground and laid my face against a rough patch of brown grass. The tips needled my skin. The flesh inside my mouth dried to the point that I thought my skin might crack open and bleed. Every one of my bones and muscles raged with fire. From the corner of my right eye, I saw solar flares detonating on the sun's surface, like yellow atomic bombs, one after the other. Julio's and Luis' phones sparked and exploded. A circular burnt area of grass was all that remained of them.

The crystals I'd hidden in my shorts turned into hot coals that burned against my skin, but I couldn't maneuver well enough to get rid of them.

We all wailed in turmoil, hoping for the twisting and turning on our bodies to end.

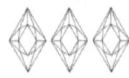

I opened my eyes and checked the time on my fancy wristwatch. It said four o' clock. Somewhere along the line, I'd fallen unconscious for almost an hour.

Losing time wasn't new to me. Such was the life of a kid who blacked out.

The others were in the same boat. Slowly they crawled to their feet. I helped Rhapsody, because she was the closest, then Esteban. Selby aided Sasha. I left them alone. Sorting that out would come later. Moving the crystals took priority.

"We've gotta get out of here," Rhapsody said, staring at one of the headstones.

No use fighting the urge to look. I read the inscription riddled with white and green mold. *Margaret Fletcher King. Beloved Wife and Mother.*

It may not have been a trap, but it sure wasn't a coincidence we were here.

"Esteban, take Rhapsody. Sasha, you go with Selby. King's coming."

Selby's mouth dropped open. "What? Are you sure?"

Sasha refused to make eye contact with me. I ignored her. "Positive," I said to them. "Go. I'll handle him myself."

"Sure you will," Selby said. They zipped away, leaving a trail of shredded grass behind them.

Esteban made his way over to Rhapsody. "Ready?"

Her eyes moistened. "I'm waiting for Jason to explain." Rhapsody's voice broke a little, so she cleared her throat. "Explain how the Collective is terrified of going up against King but he's not."

She examined my face as if the answers were hidden behind my eyes. After a month of knowing me, she'd figured me out. Truth was, my heart fluttered and I managed to again sweat past the cooling system in my suit. What good was it? I turned my head and refused to give her the satisfaction of being right.

"Live or die, Esteban, I'm staying with him."

Okay, I might not be able to take King alone, but she and Esteban couldn't do it, either, and they shouldn't have to die trying unless I failed.

I had an idea.

Grabbing Rhapsody by the waist, I planted a kiss on her. Her hot tears trailed down from her closed eyes onto my cheek as she returned my kisses. Behind her back, I used my thumb to give a "get out of here" signal to Esteban. For a brief second I opened my eyes to check his understanding. Esteban nodded. He got it.

I had to do this alone.

Slowly we drew away from each other. Rhapsody placed her hands on my cheeks and gave me a short peck. She dabbed her thumbs at the corners of my mouth.

"Goodbye." I said, stepping back.

Esteban grabbed her shoulder, and in a wisp of gold smoke they were gone.

One of the asylum's worn window shutters dropped on the overgrown thorn bush below it. I shuddered. "It's old. He wouldn't announce himself like that."

Time to get out of here before King ambushed me. I heaved the goshenite onto my left shoulder and the scarlet emerald on my right. They belonged in the pit at Hidden Potential. Maybe Vivienne had an idea of the aquamarine's whereabouts, the storm would pass, and we could all go home.

Without Rhapsody to shield me from radar, this needed to be a shorter trip. I churned enough energy inside me to go supersonic and took off.

I'm not sure from where or how, but a blast of force knocked the breath out of me and sent me spiraling out of the sky. Though I saw myself on a collision course with the earth, I didn't have the concentration to steady myself and slow down. I'm sure some kind of girlish scream came from my mouth, but at that speed I couldn't hear it.

When I struck land headfirst my momentum rolled me over into a balled-up heap. I grunted, tasting the hard orange grit between my teeth. Spitting it out didn't work. It covered my lips and the sides of my mouth. There was so much it was like I had eaten a bowl of the stuff. Would a gallon of water down my throat clear it out? And what could have hit me that hard and *that fast?* A flying bus?

Kneeling, I didn't see anything, not even a trail of smoke in the sky. A small wind blew, but not enough to make a noise on the deserted landscape. Rocky cliffs, formations – nothing else as far as the eye could see, except for the massive dust cloud I'd created when I crashed.

I rubbed the back of my neck, cracked it, and urged my reluctant feet over to the scarlet emerald first. Millions of its dark red facets sparkled in the afternoon sunlight. Goshenite would sap his powers, but with these I could enter his mind, or control his movements, like I had done to Spivey before Sasha wiped his brain clean.

Are those footsteps? Only one other person would be out here in the middle of nowhere. Instead of swinging at him, I grasped a cluster of scarlet emerald prisms.

"Freeze," I said, praying that it worked.

Turning around, I saw King. He looked like a slightly older version of the man I'd seen in the journal's photograph. Was he frozen or not? As he exhaled, his breath blew the hair on his ragged brown mustache. Otherwise, he didn't even blink.

First things first. Without goshenite nearby, I'd have to find his prisms and take them off. Most of us wore necklaces, so he probably had one, too. Only a few, like Welker, chose rings or some other type of jewelry.

I reached out for his neck to search underneath his army green collar. That's when he wrapped his hand around my throat, lifted me into the air, and flung me overhead. Hands out, I waved my arms and thought of a gliding bird. It didn't work. Every thought passed through my mind too fast to process.

When I landed, my head cracked against a rocky boulder the size of a small car. Under normal circumstances it would have broken my skull. A tiny part of me wished it had, so I could sleep, or let someone else figure out how to save the planet this time.

Maybe it did. For a minute, probably much longer than that, I lost consciousness. After gaining it back long enough to see an orange and blue blur, I dropped out again.

When I awoke, the metallic taste of blood flooded my mouth. I coughed out a stream of crimson mixed with dust. A burning, throbbing pressure invaded my sinuses. I heard a long, painful, desperate moan – *mine.*

Opening my eyes, I saw King. He knelt in front of me and dropped a denim blue name badge cracked in half into my lap. It read "Debra" – her work badge?

"She begged me not to kill you," he said with no hint of sympathy in his voice.

A lump formed in my throat. My stomach tingled with anticipation of the worst.

"So, I killed her instead." His grin seared into my brain. "You're welcome."

My brain went numb. He'd done me a "favor" and murdered my stepmom? He was lying, doing it to get me angry. Debra misplaced her badge all the time. Tears filled my eyes. No. My lip quivered. She couldn't die, not this way. Who would take care of my little brother? Who would love me?

I'd save her. I'd save them all.

Digging my right hand into the surface behind me, I tossed orange dirt into King's face. He cursed, stumbled backwards, and frantically wiped at his eyes with the sleeve of his shirt. Close as I could get, I reared back and grunted as I punched King square in the stomach. The impact lifted him several inches off of his feet. *Debra.* I saw her gentle face in my mind's eye. His entire body shook with my next punch.

Lifting him by the midsection, I threw him like a football into a nearby quarry. He'd survive it. Good. I wanted him to suffer. First, I'd take away his powers. The goshenite wasn't too far from where I threw him.

Then. . .it hit me. I'd have to kill him. No wonder Selby left so fast.

Leaping over the cracked earth to where King had landed, I battered him with my fists, holding nothing back. With every strike the control Susan had taught me to sense slipped away in small chunks. My guilt over losing it melted away, too. The smack of my fists striking against his flesh faded away to nothing.

Oh no. Not now.

I paused long enough for King to sneak in a shot at me. He tried to strangle me, digging his fingernails into the sides of my neck. I yelped, pounding away at his elbows as the pressure on my throat made me woozy. Soon my arms were heavy, like I was swinging lead pipes through liquid concrete.

We traded blow after blow. While he clearly had an effect on me, it did not seem that my efforts were worth anything beyond entertainment for him.

That was, until I noticed a drop of blood coming from his bottom lip.

I pulled King to his feet and tossed him as high as I could. We'd take it to the air, where I had an advantage on all of my enemies.

Using my hand as a visor, I tracked the black streaking dot in the sky. One thing I remembered Peters teaching us in Physical Science was something called "terminal velocity." King would meet terminal velocity, stop accelerating, and fall.

He finally slowed down and stopped at terminal velocity.

But he didn't drop. Great. He can fly and I can't.

I swallowed hard and realized my best bet was to get to the goshenite. He saw my move coming and met me in the air when I jumped for it. Even with nothing behind him for leverage, he spun me around and threw me back to the ground.

Still unable to put on the brakes, I left a crater several yards deep. I curled into a ball in a thick bed of hard, orange rubble. And this time it *really hurt*.

Had my prism flown out of my suit? No time to regroup and check. And, to be honest, I'd rather not know so far in advance if I was about to die.

King dropped down into the hole with a chunk of white ice in his hand.

CHAPTER TWENTY-SEVEN

this one's for Cherish

Straightening out my right leg helped kill the pain a bit. It was all I could do after King used the goshenite he juggled in his hand to strip me of my powers.

No one could rescue me. I couldn't be tracked without my phone or prism. None of the others knew my location. Facing King was on me. I wanted it that way, because even now only I could stop him. Since Debra had traded her life for mine, I owed her that. For better or worse, I was on my own. If I failed, at least I wouldn't have to watch my friends die torturous deaths.

He's cocky, which plays into my favor. Maniacs like to hear themselves talk, and that's not just in the movies. Plus, like everyone else, he thought I was *stupid*. The longer he rambled, the better my chance of thinking my way out of this. Without Adderall, though, it was way harder for me to focus, but at least he couldn't read my thoughts.

Sweat moistened his brow. "Unite the crystals for me and nobody else will die."

If changing sides guaranteed someone's safety, I'd do it. What was his word worth, anyway? His plan was to absorb the radiation to make himself immortal. Not for a second did I think he'd spend eternity playing chess and watching TV.

As if to make me decide faster, King stomped on my chest with his black boot and pressed the steel toe into the flesh just below my throat. "You have the potential to be an asset to me. You found the emerald."

"No," I growled beneath his shoe. "Cherish Watkins did."

He laughed. "Maybe. But you're the one who got my attention."

His statement didn't clarify whether or not he had planted a morganite jewel on her. If I made it back to Rhapsody she'd want to know, so I accused him. "You told her to shoot herself."

"She found morganite on her own. There are isotopes scattered across the globe. You can thank the Collective for that. They're as guilty as I am, if not more."

The idea that there were kids like us in other countries gave me pause. They could be unstoppable criminals, mass murderers, or worse.

King moved his foot from my chest and kicked my injured leg. I screamed and cursed from the dull ache and throbbing that came afterward.

He smiled a wicked grin and stomped me under the kneecap for good measure, causing white lights to flash in my eyes. Poking at me again with his foot, he asked me about the aquamarine. "Where did they hide it? The old lab? The HAARP compound?"

Fantastic. Welker had told him about my bluff and he'd believed it. "Ask your sister."

"Can't now," he said matter-of-factly, drawing a slow finger across his throat.

An icy shiver tickled my spine. He'd killed her, too.

He leaned over me and pressed the goshenite against my ribs near the bottom of my good lung. Shaking my head back and forth, I wanted to shout but couldn't find the breath to do it. I'm sure my face purpled from a lack of oxygen, which led King to let up on the pressure.

He scratched at his stubble. Something in his beady eyes told me time was running short, so I had to think quicker. "The aquamarine's location," he growled. "*Now.*"

Could I sell him on a fake site? Probably not. I thought "I don't know," but with a collapsed lung and the inability to speak, I mouthed it.

My hesitation must have convinced him I really didn't know. King balled his right fist and cocked his arm back to strike me dead. I closed my eyes, ready to allow it to happen. I couldn't fight anymore, not without help.

When King didn't immediately hit me, I cracked open my eyes. He dropped the white rock and staggered, falling backwards and gurgling spit on himself.

"I don't know," I croaked between coughs. "Happy?"

Wide-eyed and shaking, King keeled over and clutched at his stomach.

Lying on my back, I watched the milder light of the afternoon sun filter through the clouds. Humongous solar flares blew up across its surface, one after the other. For the moment my enemy was powerless and unable to defend himself against me. The goshenite was closer than I thought, about three yards away. I'd have to look for the scarlet emerald, but by the time I found it the solar flares would be over.

Rolling over to King, I searched his shirt and pants for any color of prism. He halfheartedly pushed me away until I delivered a couple hard punches to his jaw.

We weren't done – not even close.

Once he stopped moving I concentrated on searching him while the flares were still going. His pockets were clean. Where was he keeping them? I experienced a small surge of energy with them being so close, but any more power and I'd be sick like he was.

Against my better judgment, I tore open his clothes and stripped him down to his white tank top and pale blue boxer shorts.

Not one prism.

One look at the sun let me know that the flares were weakening. I broke out in a cold sweat in the middle of the desert. King's strength would return soon. "C'mon, think!" I said, smacking my head with my hands.

My eyes wandered across his body, even the places I didn't *want* to look. Then in the sunlight, I saw a faint glimmer on the left side of his chest.

Unzipping my suit and pulling my arms free from the sleeves, I touched the hairy area above his heart. A hard sharpness pricked me. On closer examination, I saw a loose flap of leathery skin.

Gross. He implanted them.

King groaned and blinked his eyes. I grabbed the goshenite rock, suppressed his powers, and continued my search as the solar storm ended as quickly as it had begun.

Using my fingernails, I dug underneath the flap of skin on his sweaty chest. I pulled out five small prisms – the green emerald, then the goshenite, scarlet emerald, morganite, and heliodor.

I pocketed the green emerald and immediately revived. With the remaining four crystals in my hand, I stepped far enough away that King could not draw power from them. His skin sagged, darkened, and withered on his bones.

He gagged and hacked, clutching at his throat. "Noooo," he wailed.

An uncontrollable desire to break him in half rose within me. I told him the first word on my mind, "Die." He was way too dangerous to survive. Of all the people who tried to kill me – Peters, Selby, Welker, and now him – King is the only one for whom I wanted to return the favor.

I gazed at his wretched body long and hard. What kind of end did he deserve?

I remembered the morganite, the one stone that would not revive or sustain him. I flung the fingernail-sized prism next to his arm. "That's for Cherish and Debra," I said.

King twitched with surprise and patted the ground until he found the crystal. Holding it close to his face, for his eyesight must have worsened, he laughed. Not at my stupidity for leaving him a prism, but the fact he'd done the same thing to us.

Whatever his deepest desire might be, he'd discover it here, alone in the desert with his last breath. Eventually he'd want to die bad enough to find a way to do it.

He deserved it for all he'd done.

When I landed at Hidden Potential after six o'clock, the ground was scorching, like beach sand. Rhapsody waited for me beside the pit. No one else hung around.

After I unloaded the scarlet emerald and goshenite crystals from my shoulders onto the ground, Rhapsody rushed into my arms and gave me a kiss. In the middle of the kiss, I fell to my knees and broke into tears. She eased back and held me tight. I wanted to tell her everything, that King had murdered my only real parent and I'd left him to die for it. My mouth wouldn't form the words or anything beyond a pitiful wail.

"What happened? Whatever it is, no judgment. You can tell me."

"Debra," I sobbed.

Rhapsody read between the lines. She placed her hands on my neck and looked at me while I bowed my head.

"He killed her. . ."

"When this is all over, Jason, we'll find out the truth." Her voice rose in pitch. "Did you. . ."

"No."

She touched my cheeks with her palms. "And don't leave me like that again."

"Promise," I said, holding my hand up in a pledge. "I had a good excuse though."

Heat from the pit pulsed through the soil and created small pockets of hissing steam. Something wasn't right.

The solar storm wasn't supposed to peak until noon tomorrow.

"It's been doing this for the past half hour," Rhapsody said as we stood. "Vivienne told us to take off our prisms if we see solar flares coming, but they're hard to get a jump on."

I lifted the lid to the pit and a gush of boiling air puffed up at me. I dropped the scarlet emerald inside, then the goshenite. The prisms I'd stolen from King were next. Then I resealed the pit's cover.

"What's wrong?" she asked me.

"Nothing," I said, forcing a smile from my sweaty face. "I'm good."

Rhapsody crossed her arms over her breasts. "You don't wanna talk about it. It's fine. You know me. I won't force you."

It's one of the things about her I appreciated the most.

"What if the solar storm is coming quicker, harder than we think? Nobody knows where the aquamarine is, not King, not even the Collective – or so they said."

She sighed. "We've got most of them. The pit will hold those, won't it?"

"And what if it doesn't?" I asked. "What if the whole thing blows?"

"I don't know, Jason," she said. "What do you think we should do?"

Our time was winding down. Whether I believed King or not, the Collective wasn't telling us everything. I'd force them to tell me the rest.

CHAPTER TWENTY-EIGHT

we all make sacrifices

Nobody smart leaves five nuclear bombs unattended.

Probably remembering the last time we'd parted company, Rhapsody refused to leave my side. "It won't be long before Vivienne comes back," she said.

The Collective? I didn't trust them. "Alright," I said.

We sat next to each other on the coolest part of the ground adjacent to the pit. All around us the angry earth bubbled and popped, sending fragments of hot dirt into the air. The heat didn't bother me, but it scalded Rhapsody. She found a patch of grass to sit on and twirled her hair around her fingers.

"What's up with you and Girl Genius?" she asked me after a long silence. "There's really no good time to ask. . ."

Keeping in mind we could easily die in the next twenty-four hours, I was honest. "Is she into Selby again, or something?"

Rhapsody squinted and made a sound like she was hurt. "They disappeared from camp together after you left. Who knows?"

Maybe they're making another video. "I can't even deal with them right now."

"Gotcha," she said with a hint of regret in her voice. "Nuclear apocalypse first."

Soon we saw Vivienne running towards us. Hughes, Courtney, Camuto. and Peters were with her. Esteban was behind them. Where was Welker?

"You made it back," Esteban said when they were within earshot.

I scratched the back of my head. "Don't sound so surprised."

"What did you do to David?" Vivienne asked. She sounded like she cared.

"He murdered my stepmother." I deadpanned. "I'm fine, thanks for asking."

"Sorry," Vivienne said, shrugging. She still expected an answer.

"I did to him the same thing you all did to Cherish Watkins," I said.

Vivienne gasped. *Did she figure out what King told me about the prisms they had left across the planet?* "Oh," she said with relief. "So you *didn't* kill him?"

"No," I admitted.

Esteban laughed. "Good move."

The area rumbled with a series of violent tremors that shook us to the ground. Courtney fell on a geyser of steam and screamed, holding the scalded skin on her back.

Hughes helped Courtney back to her feet. "Did you find the aquamarine?" he asked me. "We're running out of time."

"Too busy fighting your old friend," I said to him. "Are you sure Vivienne's containment field isn't going to fail? Maybe I should get the one from the HAARP compound."

The color drained out of Camuto's face. Peters paled, as well.

Oh no. It was happening.

The solar storm ravaged the sun's surface. Layers of emerald green, royal purple, hot pink, and sunset orange light rippled across the atmosphere. Although we were less than an hour from sunset, the colorful sky lit up like the middle of the day. Northern lights occurring on this part of the planet weren't normal. Our bodies must have adjusted to the radiation increases. I didn't collapse in pain anymore. Neither did the others.

"The storm is in its main phase now," Hughes said.

Esteban raised his eyebrows. "Uhh. . .i-it's not supposed to do that until midday tomorrow, is it?"

The storm was early, *way early*. Rhapsody, Esteban, and I were surprised, but our "benefactors" weren't.

"Wait, you knew this was going to happen!" Rhapsody screamed at the Collective. "You weren't going to tell us? So we just cross our fingers now and hope the planet doesn't cut in half?"

Courtney had been friendlier to us, so I approached her. "Where is it?" I asked. "You knew where the heliodor was all this time. Where is the aquamarine?"

She turned to Vivienne. "Do you know?" she asked her. "He's our only chance."

Vivienne's lips trembled. "Belinda and I. . .we hid the aquamarine in your town. An abandoned chemical plant. . .it's in a foundation beam. . .the northeast corner."

Rhapsody smacked my shoulder. We both were thinking the same thing.

We mumbled out the name of the plant where our parents used to work.

Vivienne nodded. "Yes. That's the place."

The muscles in my face, neck and arms tensed. I paced in circles and cursed at her until spit flew out of my mouth with every word.

"Is there a reason? Other than slowly killing our parents from cancer, I mean. Is there another reason why you waited this long to say something?" Rhapsody asked Vivienne.

"Because of what it does," Vivienne said solemnly. "Belinda and I knew the anarchy David would have created with it. We had to keep it hidden until. . ."

They never thought I was going to beat him. "I'm going," I said, interrupting her.

Esteban stepped forward and carefully approached me. "You're needed here. Let me go in your place."

It was true. I was the invulnerable one, the last chance to catch the spiking radiation. Would I die when I absorbed it? If I didn't, wouldn't everyone else?

"Alright," I said with resignation. "How will you get it out of concrete?"

Rhapsody cleared her throat. "He'll take me along. I can ghost it out."

Every worst case scenario flashed in my head, where it explodes and they both go with it. Another tremor shook the ground for a few seconds and hot steam shot into the air. Its temperature had to be way over one hundred degrees.

Peters peeked over at the pit and cursed. "I hate it when David's right."

I dropped my chin to my chest. Vivienne's pit had broken open.

Rhapsody came close to me. Maybe I was hallucinating but I swore I could still smell her perfume. She placed her hands on my chest. They were shaking, so I used my hands to steady them.

"I suck at goodbyes." She looked down at her feet.

I squeezed her hands. "Then come back and you won't have to say it."

We hugged and I sneaked a kiss on her cheek. She whispered something in Spanish in my ear. She must have figured she'd have to come back to translate it for me.

Esteban waved to us before teleporting them in a puff of golden smoke. Depending on how far he could go per transport, they could be away for a while.

Peters grabbed my forearm and pointed to the pit. "It might blow soon."

I looked at him, with no choice but to have faith in whatever he told me. "Am I coming out of this? Will I be okay?"

His eyes flitted back and forth, as if he was calculating the odds in his head. "I don't know, Jason. None of us do. It's King's theory, not mine."

"And no theory becomes truth without a test," I said.

Peters patted me on the back. "Good luck," he said.

Obviously I couldn't wait for Esteban and Rhapsody to return. Though the sun was less than an hour from going down, the crystals were reaching a critical stage. The flares were ongoing and getting bigger.

Whoever coined the phrase "it's hot as Hell" must have stood next to a pit full of nuclear radiation. The heat didn't burn me, but I was uncomfortable in it. Courtney attempted to say something to me before I jumped inside, but I didn't want to hear it.

There was no explanation she could give for what Vivienne and Belinda had done to make it okay. Their game of "Keep Away" with King had given George and my mom incurable bone cancer. No wonder George had a hissy fit when he saw the green emeralds. He must have seen the aquamarine somehow. *How many others had died because of them?*

"Jason!" Camuto yelled at me as I closed in on the pit. "Thank you."

"For what?" I screamed over the hissing steam fountains.

"For saving us," she said. "For saving *me.*"

I nodded. Lifting the lid, I eased down into the pit and closed it myself.

How long I was down in the pit was impossible to tell – minutes, hours. At the worst, the humming of the energy was deafening, but eventually it tailed off.

I actually fell in and out of sleep in there. The heat didn't seem to be hot anymore. It was comforting, almost cool. My heartbeat, which throbbed in my ears at one point, was quiet to the point of nonexistence.

I waved my arms and moved my legs around in the pit, which was large enough for me to stretch out around the jutting stones. They were light and weightless. I shouted up toward the lid, "I'm okay," but I had no voice. I plugged my ears with my fingers and tried again so I could hear inside my head. Nope, no voice.

Suddenly the energy of all five crystals pulsed to a fevered pitch. Their humming reached the sound levels of a jet engine. Gusts of hot wind shot up from the bottom of the pit. Rhapsody and Esteban were too late.

This is it. I maneuvered over to the crack in the side of the pit. It was almost exactly the width of my body. I spread my limbs out, making a giant letter "X" over it. I believed Rhapsody and Esteban would appear in the next few seconds. They'd dump the aquamarine crystal down onto me, and I'd shield them from its energy, too.

Cocooned by blinding light, I said a quick prayer for my soul and closed my eyes a split second before the explosion.

CHAPTER TWENTY-NINE

sophomore freak

I remember lying on the pit's crack and feeling like a piece of human barbecue. The radiation burned through my body like nothing I've ever experienced. A bath on the sun, perhaps, or a sauna in Hell? Something like that.

Then, just as quickly, peaceful waves of coolness washed over me. No pain or any other sense of feeling. I blinked my eyes, seeing nothing but whiteness, no shades or colors. Heaven should be white. Our pastor talked about Jesus and whiteness, like snow. Every Sunday I'd drifted off during the sermon, or I'd started thinking about food. It was amazing I remembered that much about church service.

Mom? Debra? No sound came from my numb throat. Was I dead?

Through the fuzzy white cotton wrapped around my memory, I recall opening my eyes to another brilliant light. Not white, but closer to a yellowish orange. Like the irises of a nocturnal animal, almost artificial. I stared it down, trying to figure out its origin and shape, until its brilliance burned my eyes.

I inhaled, and my right lung was sore but *functioning.* My bad leg was wrapped in something heavy, bandaged and cold.

So I'm not dead after all.

Closing my eyelids, I started sorting through things. The solar storm had happened. The heliodor, morganite, goshenite, scarlet emerald and green emerald provenance crystals had detonated beneath me. Nobody had known what would happen when they did, but I had survived it. If the world had split in half, I was on the remaining piece.

What about the radiation? Did it escape?

The first true time I woke up it was in a hospital bed. Not North Hospital, somewhere else. An auburn-haired phlebotomist came to my room to take my blood. When she opened the blinds to let light in I pretended to be asleep. My window didn't open up to anything I recognized. Rain pitter-pattered against the glass, drawing trails and patterns. Drowsy, I nodded off again. I wasn't sure for how long.

My body tensed. Looking around, all I saw were wood panels in the room. Rhapsody sat at my left side and jumped when I moved. From the deep wrinkles in her black Sex Pistols t-shirt and the tired look in her eyes, I figured she had been with me for a while. She gently stroked my hand and tried not to cry, but couldn't stop herself.

Now we didn't have to say goodbye.

"Welcome back," she sniffled, sounding like she had practiced what she would say. She clutched my fingers and laced them in hers. "Don't touch your throat."

Of course I wanted to do it, which is why she held onto my hand. Bending my left arm would compress the IV needle in it, which she would know. To satisfy my curiosity, she used the front-facing camera on her new phone to show me why I shouldn't bother.

Everything on my face looked okay, except for a small cut to my lip and a bandage taped to my neck. A horde of mosquitoes biting me on that exact spot would itch less than this.

Rhapsody dabbed the back of her hand at her running mascara. "You were on a ventilator for a while."

A while? How long? Sighing, I rolled my head to the other side of the bed. Debra wasn't there, although I half expected her to be. She had been there for most of the hard times in my life. Now she was gone. My bottom lip trembled and I fought back the tears.

What about the aquamarine? I wouldn't try talking, but I mouthed it to Rhapsody and squeezed her hand until she got the message. She looked up and I heard the door open and quickly close.

"He's awake," Rhapsody said, waving to somebody on my right. Out of the corner of my eye, I spotted Courtney, alive and well. She had been present at ground zero, so Hughes and Camuto must be okay, too.

Courtney eased into the empty chair next to Rhapsody and cleared her throat. "When you wear prisms as long as we have, your body builds up a reserve of radiation," she said in a rocky voice. "Thank you. We owe you our lives."

My eyes narrowed at the sight of her. Hate filled my insides, for her and everything she and the others had done. Besides, I hadn't saved everyone. Debra died and there was still the matter of all of those crystals the Collective left across the globe.

She scooted her chair closer to me and leaned over. The fabric of her white button-down shirt gapped enough for me to spot her heliodor necklace. "You're safe."

Remembering her definition of "safe" – that we were more powerful than our enemies – didn't comfort me. After all, like most of my other fights I'd lucked out against King – he'd almost killed me. And if she'd had a reserve, hadn't he? What if he'd survived, after all?

"Your body absorbed the worst of the explosion's radiation. We contained the rest. It was touch and go with you for a while."

Rhapsody answered before I could ask. "You've been in a coma one day and thirteen hours short of three weeks."

It was worth it, only if King was truly dead.

"While you were out," Rhapsody said, "they fixed your lung, your ACL and PCL ligaments, and the gunshot wounds to your chest. Ray. . .he paid for it all, Debra, too."

Debra, too? My heart monitor's beeping upticked. Oh, God, her funeral?

"Easy, Jason," Courtney reassured me. "Her neck is broken, but she's breathing."

My tense body relaxed. She was alive, even if Ray had something to do with it. I'd stay home, get home-schooled, and help her get better, if that's what it took.

"Explanation," I groaned. My voice had gotten deeper, and not in a good way.

Courtney ran a hand through her thick blonde hair. "There's time for that."

Rhapsody made eye contact with me. Being around Courtney wasn't acceptance for her, it was *tolerance.* She and the Collective had poisoned countless people. They'd buried the aquamarine underneath the plant. Their hands were dirty with our parents' blood.

"It wasn't a chemical plant when we buried it there," Courtney assured us.

It didn't help. What about the aquamarine now? I moved my mouth to pronounce the word, but couldn't.

"It exploded," she said. "We didn't get there in time."

If she finished another one of my thoughts, I'd think she was reading my mind. It exploded? There had to be consequences, effects, problems that had to be solved. . .

"Nobody died," Courtney said. "But we have work to do."

We?

She dug in her purse and pulled out a new necklace for me. On it were diamond-shaped prisms in all five colors – even the aquamarine, which sparkled a little brighter than the others. No morganite, which was good.

I didn't get it. Weren't the blue prisms supposed to do something awful, cause anarchy? Why would she give them to me? Better yet, why would I want them?

"The necklace is reinforced tungsten," Courtney said. "I'll wait until you're released from here to give it to you. Miracle recoveries are investigative news pieces waiting to happen. You never know who's watching."

Like the Collective, who had been watching us far longer than I thought? Without my new necklace I'd have no chance of defending my loved ones, or holding the Collective responsible for what they'd done. I'm sure my best friend would want to do the same.

"Here, you'll need this, too." Rhapsody unfolded a white piece of paper in front of my face. At the top it read *Champion, Jr., Jason Ray. North High Schedule for 2013-2014 School Year. Grade 10.*

"Great," I moaned. *I actually made it to tenth grade.*

"We have three classes together and the same lunch," she said, *"but* you'll have homeroom with Sasha."

I'd left things with her unresolved, but Rhapsody and I weren't on pause. She understood that, I think. That reminded me of what she'd said to me before the pit exploded. I think I knew, but I wasn't sure. "What's *te amo* mean?"

Rhapsody blushed and looked down. "You're such a gringo."

That was true, I guess. "I'm. . .normal."

Rhapsody tapped my left hand. "Nope. Still a *freak.*"

I thought about it for a second. I'm good with that.

THE END

Discover more by Brian Thompson:

After his latest fight, Jason Champion is sent to a rundown alternative school, nicknamed "Reject High."

Rhapsody Lowe shows Jason a crystal that turns her invisible. Jason tries one on and he *jumps over a city.*

With eleven days until Reject High is destroyed, Jason and his friends must dodge their pursuers and save their power source from falling into the wrong hands.

ISBN: 978-0-989-10560-6 * Paperback * 270 pages
Available in electronic format at www.amazon.com

www.greatnationpublishing.com

After a failed coup, a revolutionary named Noor is exiled to earth and sentenced to death. He vows to rule the inferior planet.

In the year 2050, tragedy strikes Harper Lowe, Damario Coley, Quinne Ruiz, and Teanna Kirkwood. Through the Genesis Institute, they are all offered the chance to "begin again."

When the project's true motives are revealed, the group is sent hurtling toward an uncertain future with unpredictable consequences.

ISBN: 978-0-615-60216-1 * Paperback * 264 pages
Available in electronic format at www.amazon.com

www.greatnationpublishing.com

www.ingramcontent.com/pod-product-compliance
Lightning Source LLC
Chambersburg PA
CBHW020727210626
46807CB00016B/370